SILENC

A BOW STREE
BO

CARA DEVLIN

CHAPTER
ONE

November 1819
London

T he offices at number four Bow Street were an entirely different beast once the sun slipped behind the city's western horizon. During daylight hours, the magistrate's offices were generally sedate, with patrolmen either clearing out the overnight arrests or readying them for hearings at the magistrate's court. Come nightfall, however, those patrolmen started dragging in all manner of criminals, from petty thieves and pickpockets to drunken belligerents and unruly cyprians.

As a principal officer, Hugh Marsden no longer prowled the streets to catch criminals in the act or answer the hue and cry of wronged citizens. He was accountable for more significant arrests and investigations that took time and patience to solve. Murders were, by and large, simple things to crack as most people did a rather shoddy job of covering up their evil deeds.

People were sloppy. They were guileless and unoriginal. In short, they were predictable, which made Hugh's work relatively straightforward and boring.

However, some cases broke the mold and diverged from the ordinary and mundane.

Last April, and then again in August, Hugh had come upon two such cases. In the spring, a mutilated opera singer had been found in Seven Dials with a delirious and blood-covered man nearby, the murder weapon at his side. The fact that the man had been a duke of the realm had only further convinced Hugh that whether one lived in the East End slums, or in Mayfair, people were simple creatures.

There were exceptions, of course.

The duke's wife, Audrey Sinclair, was certainly one. She'd challenged Hugh's accusations against the duke, and rejecting the clear-cut case, she went about hunting down the true murderer, going against the grain and in the end, proving Hugh wrong. And then in August, the duchess had beckoned him to the countryside to investigate a woman's death. The unraveling of that case had been anything but straightforward, and once again, Audrey managed to untangle a host of well-concealed lies while in lockstep with Hugh.

In the near two months since that case in Hertfordshire, Hugh had made arrests in several more killings in London, none of them very inventive or complex. And most of his investigating tended to happen during the day, when the Bow Street offices resembled a busy but orderly business firm.

Tonight, however, as he entered the offices near midnight, his eyes burning from lack of sleep and his mind slightly hazed from one too many drams of whisky, Hugh remembered the hassle of working at this hour. He pitied the night officers and patrolmen. The main room was a madhouse of shouting and jostling bodies. A pair of drunken women screeched lewd and suggestive comments at the harried booking officer behind the front desk while several patrolmen attempted to keep a group of ragtags from entering fisticuffs. An old woman with black-ened gums and hardly any teeth laughed hysterically as she bounced a wailing baby, bundled in fouled linens, upon her knee. And to top it off, in the corner, a stray, mangy dog lifted its leg over a potted plant.

Immediately, Hugh regretted his decision to leave his warm, quiet home on Bedford Street at such a ridiculous hour. He had no one to blame but himself. It wasn't as if he'd been summoned to the station, and earlier that afternoon, he'd resolved an investigation into several stolen shipments of snuff (an assistant to the tobacconist who reported the theft had, unsurprisingly, thought to sell it for his own gain). Hugh had but some papers to sort through and reports to complete for filing. Nothing that could not wait until proper morning.

However, Bow Street had been a better alternative to lying awake in bed until dawn, dwelling on what Miss Gloria Hanson had whispered in his ear that evening as they lay side-by-side, sweaty and spent: *"Who were you just making love to? It was not me."*

He'd stared at his long-standing mistress, baffled, and asked her to explain her meaning. Though now, he wished he had not.

The harassed booking officer caught Hugh's eye. He parted his lips, as if to call to him, and Hugh quickly raised a hand in greeting before darting toward his office. Once inside, he closed the door, shutting out the chaos. He hung his greatcoat and top hat, both damp from a misty autumn rain, and sighed as he collapsed into the creaky chair behind his desk. The room was small and windowless, likely a closet when the building had been a residence during the previous century, before Sir Henry

Fielding had founded the Runners. But it was his own space, and for that, Hugh was grateful.

He leaned back into the chair and stared at the stacks of waiting files on his blotter. Then, sighed heavily. It seemed all he'd managed to do was change his physical location, for the memory of Gloria's bold question continued to plague him.

"You've been different lately," she'd elaborated with an insouciant shrug of her bare shoulder.

"In what manner?"

"Distant. Like you are thinking of something else. And yet..." She had searched for the right words before settling upon, "You are also more passionate. Desperately so."

Hugh had increased their once-weekly assignations to twice-weekly, and it had not escaped him that most recently, he had been asking her to visit a third time. Their exclusive arrangement seemed to please them both.

As an assistant to Madam Gascoigne, one of the best modistes in London, Gloria earned a decent wage, however there was no question her agreement with Hugh benefited her greatly. And while most men of Hugh's circumstances would not bother to keep a regular mistress and would instead spread their seed among the many willing ladies of the *demimonde*, or even among lower-class cyprians, that sort of transaction had never appealed to him. Instead, for the last year, Gloria had warmed his bed. Apparently, she had keen skills of observation.

"I apologize if I have failed to satisfy," he'd said, sitting up in bed and eyeing the clock with an unexpected urge to flee. That usually didn't happen. Gloria's company was comfortable, and it tended to keep his mind from wandering toward thoughts and people that did him no good.

"Never that," she replied in her familiar composed and unaffected tone. He had always appreciated that about her.

Emotions were not part of their relationship. "But lately, there is something...impatient about you."

"Desperate *and* impatient, is it? Safe to say my ego is wounded."

She huffed. "You make love to me like someone is trying to rip me away from you."

Hugh had thrown off the blanket and gotten dressed. He had no idea what to say to that. Gloria must have decided that to continue the conversation would be disadvantageous, for she dressed as well. Not even a word in parting when she kissed his cheek before leaving.

Who are you making love to?

Hugh sat forward, bracing his elbows upon the desk, and scrubbed his palm over his eyes. Three drams of whisky had not dulled his mind or made him at all sleepy, but perhaps this paperwork would.

A knock landed on his closed door as he picked up a folio and untoggled it.

"Enter," he called, knowing he sounded gruff but secretly welcoming the distraction.

One of the senior patrol officers stepped in, his clothing drenched from the waist down. His uniform's blue tailcoat dripped a trail of water upon the floor.

Hugh frowned and guessed at the man's plight. "Not the finest night for a wade into the Thames, is it, Stevens?"

"It is not," he agreed.

"A body?"

"Yes, sir."

Hugh waited for the officer to say more, but Stevens's lips were twisted into a contemplative grimace. He had some sympathy for the young man. Hugh had pulled many a corpse from the river during his time on street patrol. The fresh ones were not always so bad, but the ones that had been left in the mud and water to age a bit were a trial to look upon. To smell, too. Often, the skin bloated to something grotesque, discolored to a putrid green, and at times would even split open. It was not uncommon for the little critters in the river to begin feasting either. It turned his stomach just thinking of it.

"Is there something I can help you with, Stevens?" Hugh pressed as the man stood there for a few more protracted moments. His skin appeared paler than usual, and a bit waxen.

He cleared his throat. "It's, ah... Well, I was about to send someone to Bedford Street to fetch you, sir. But Davis said you were here."

Davis, the beleaguered booking officer he had effectively dodged.

"Why send for me?" Hugh asked. And near midnight, at that. A dead body could surely wait in the bone house until morning.

"I don't quite know how to... You see, it's..." Stevens cleared his throat again, took something silver from his tailcoat's pocket, and then crossed the room. He set the object on the desk.

"A calling card case?" Hugh eyed the silver filigree lid, centered with an enamel posy of violets. He picked it up and sprang the latch. Inside was a clump of damp cardstock.

Just as he was deducing that the object had been found with the drowned body, he read the engraved contents of the top card.

Hugh went still. He stared at the card, then snapped his eyes to Stevens. "What is the meaning of this?"

The patrolman swallowed visibly. "Sir, the item was found in the skirt pocket of the woman we pulled from the river."

Hugh dropped the case onto the desk and pushed back his chair. The room spun around him, growing smaller. He heard the patrolman's voice continuing to explain that as soon he found the calling cards he immediately thought of Principal Officer Marsden—and that it might be best if he be the one to inform His Grace, the Duke of Fournier.

Hugh shot to his feet. "It is not her. It cannot be. Bring me to the body."

Stevens's eyes rounded. "You don't want to see it, sir. It's bad off, and she's...well, the face is..." He shook his head and suffered a bout of shivers. "You wouldn't recognize it."

Hugh stared at the card case. His ears began to chime. His whole body thrummed with the need to move, to run, to do *something*.

The body they'd fished out of the Thames was not Audrey's.

Despite what the calling cards said, it could not be the Duchess of Fournier.

He had not seen her for two months, not since leaving Fournier Downs in Hertfordshire. He had no idea what she had been doing or whom she had interacted with. Other members of polite society to be sure, as there was no reason for her to socialize with anyone else. Especially someone from Hugh's level of society, which really wasn't considered society at all. But she had a habit of being reckless when she got a bee in her bonnet about something. Had she stumbled across another potential crime? Met someone unsavory? Hugh's heart rate increased, and a cold sweat formed under his clothing as he pocketed the card case and dismissed Stevens.

"Will you visit the duke?" the patrolman inquired as Hugh grabbed his greatcoat and hat.

He might have replied, but he couldn't be sure. He wasn't completely aware of the next several moments, for the next thing Hugh knew, he was on the street, hailing a hack. Violet House, Fournier's London home, was in Mayfair, an area of town he usually had no call to frequent. At this hour, just past midnight, the streets near Hyde Park would be nearly empty.

The rain-slicked roads glimmered yellow by the light of the gas jets in the lampposts. It was well past proper calling hours, but there was no impropriety Hugh could possibly care enough about right then to stop him.

The weight of the silver case was an anchor in his pocket as the jarvey directed the hack along Curzon Street. All ladies and gentlemen presented their cards when calling upon another member of society whom they were not already familiar with. These cards were as much a form of identification as they were a social courtesy. The footman at the door would accept the card and present it to their employer, who would then decide whether they were in or out.

How could Audrey's case have found its way into another woman's reticule?

He closed his eyes and, for what could have been the hundredth or thousandth time, returned to the old citrine quarry at Fournier Downs. Hugh had just come to Audrey's aid on the narrow jutting ledges of the open quarry pit. She'd fallen from the edge above and by pure luck had struck one of the craggy shelves instead of tumbling to her death some seventy feet below, onto rocky debris. He had been reeling with relief and gratitude that she was still alive, and in that moment of vulnerability, had nearly given in to the desire he'd been trying to bury since April. He'd come so close to kissing her that he'd felt her breath upon his lips. Thankfully, the duke had shouted from above, wrenching them apart.

As it should have been.

Kissing her would have been a gargantuan mistake, but try as he had, Hugh could not wipe the inane desire from where it had settled under his very skin.

The hack came to a stop out front of Violet House. An ill sweep of dread flooded his stomach as he tossed the jarvey his fare and then started toward the darkened front steps. He brought down the brass knocker three times and waited, knowing such a late-hour call would cause a ruckus. Arriving home past midnight would not be uncommon for the duke and duchess, if they had been attending the theatre or a ball. But had they been out, the exterior lamps would have been left burning and the front windows would have been bright with candlelight to welcome them home. A footman would also have been stationed near the front door to allow them in without delay. As Hugh stood waiting for a full minute, forced to employ the door-knocker once again, he concluded the house was simply asleep.

Finally, footsteps approached. Locks turned. The door opened to reveal a disheveled footman, a livery coat thrown over his sleeping clothes and his powdered wig askew.

"Sir?" he blurted out wearily.

"Officer Hugh Marsden with Bow Street. I need to speak to the duke. Immediately."

The footman began to stammer a reply about the time of night and the duke being indisposed, but Hugh cut him off. "Understand that this is an emergency. It involves the duchess." His throat cinched around the words.

A light appeared at the top of the staircase. "Marsden? Is that you? At this hour. What the devil—?"

Robed and fresh from his bedchamber, the duke descended the carpeted steps holding a candle. The footman stepped aside, and Hugh entered the foyer.

"Your Grace, I—" Hugh faltered. Cleared his throat. "I'm afraid I must ask...when was the last you saw the duchess?"

Fournier came to a stop on the last step and scowled. "What kind of question is that? It is past midnight, Marsden. Are you drunk?"

"I am not drunk," he bit off, barbs of irritation sharpening.

9

"I am aware of the time. I've just come from Bow Street. There has been a...a body. Pulled from the Thames."

"What does that have to do with me? Or my wife?" Fournier held the candle in its holder higher, as if to inspect Hugh for any sign of drunkenness.

He swallowed what felt like shards of broken glass. "I have reason to believe it could be—"

"Hugh?"

Her voice reached him before a second candle on the upstairs landing registered in his vision. Dismissing the duke and footman, and propriety altogether, Hugh went to the base of the stairs and gripped the carved wooden newel post. Audrey came down the steps, her hair draped over her shoulder in a thick blond plait, a banyan cinched around her waist. Her lips were parted, her cheeks rosy from sleep. She looked beautiful—and unequivocally alive.

"Mr. Marsden," she said, correcting the familiar uttering of his name, which she had likely done out of surprise at seeing him in her foyer. "What is happening?"

He closed his eyes and exhaled, a hundred stone lifting from his chest. "It is not you."

"What isn't me?"

"A dead body, I presume," the duke said tightly, his patience thinning rapidly. "You best explain yourself, Marsden."

The duke could have launched into a vitriolic diatribe right then, and Hugh would not have cared. The body Stevens found was not Audrey's. He nearly swayed on his feet with relief. She stood before him on the stairs, her eyes shining with concern in the dim candlelight.

He reached into his pocket and revealed the silver calling card case.

She took another few steps toward him, her eyes locked on the case, her hand reaching for it. "Where did you find that?"

"A patrolman fished a woman out of the Thames tonight. This was in the waist pocket ," he answered.

She quickly retracted her hand, leaving the case in his palm. She didn't wish to touch it, and Hugh thought he knew why. Objects held onto memories; memories that Audrey could see in her fascinating mind whenever she touched them. She would not wish to see whatever memories this object retained.

She frowned, her brows pinched together as if in confusion.

"I misplaced this case weeks ago," she said, shaking her head. "I don't understand, how did it get into the pocket of a—"

Her brow smoothed, and her lips parted on a gust of air. She stared at the case in his hand with dawning recognition.

"*Oh.* Oh no. I think I know who the dead woman is."

CHAPTER
TWO

"You should have left this to me," Philip grumbled as their carriage traveled the near-empty streets toward the dead house. "There is no reason for you to subject yourself to this."

Audrey held her tongue, if only because of their guest. Principal Officer Hugh Marsden sat across from her and Philip in the brougham, and he too seemed to be biting his tongue. Hugh hadn't said much since she realized whose body the Bow Street patrolman must have pulled from the waters of the Thames.

He'd listened to her explanation and then, when she asked to see the body, he'd given a firm nod of understanding. Unlike Philip.

"If it is Delia, I need to be certain," she now replied.

"I cannot believe you kept her visits from me." The duke's tone, taut with displeasure, sounded like a reprimand from a peeved nanny. She refrained from rolling her eyes and instead, stared at the darkened window.

Audrey had her reasons for keeping Delia's visits a secret, and not just because her husband would have deterred the young woman from coming to Violet House. Audrey could not truthfully say she had enjoyed Delia's visits either, but she had felt a duty to her. A comradery, even. She and Delia shared a past—one they had both been trying to put behind them.

Audrey chose not to defend herself, at least not for now. She would not quarrel with her husband in front of Hugh. It was already uncomfortable enough sitting within the same carriage, the three of them together.

When she saw Hugh standing within the foyer of Violet House, it was as though the last two months—which had passed glacially—had suddenly been nothing but a blink of time. The Little Season was firmly underway in London, with dinners, concerts, balls, and routs to attend nearly every night of the week. But even with her busy schedule, Audrey felt each week limping along, farther and farther away from the week in Hertfordshire when Hugh had helped her hunt down a murderer. That investigation had ended with Audrey's near demise—and with Hugh nearly kissing her as they stood precariously on a ledge in a quarry pit.

The unbidden, soaring thrill of seeing him again, of remembering his lips, so close to hers, had almost completely snuffed out when she comprehended the only reason he could have for a midnight visit.

"Identification could be difficult, considering the supposed state of the remains," Hugh said gravely. "The patrolmen who retrieved it suggested the face was...greatly deteriorated."

Philip made a low sound in his throat, and Audrey, too, felt a spike of repulsion.

Hugh had believed the body to be *hers*, she now understood, and after rushing to dress and prepare herself for an outing to the dead house near the river, Audrey was now just beginning to contemplate the way he had gripped the newel post at the base of the staircase when he saw her. He had, for a short while, believed she was dead. His trip to Violet House had been to verify that she was missing and to inform the duke of the body found in the water. The calling card case was, after all, ample evidence. Hugh had not been able to mask his relief at finding her alive and well, and she could not stop the flutter of sentiment in her chest that he had worried so.

"I would like to see the gown at the very least," Audrey said.

"Because you believe it is your own?" Hugh was only repeating what she had hastily explained before leaving Curzon Street.

"Yes, I've given Delia a few of my cast-offs. Greer sometimes takes them too, to sell, but she prefers my simpler gowns. Delia always adored the more elaborate ones."

Audrey could not even imagine her lady's maid, Greer, wearing one of her old ball gowns, but Delia...she had fawned over them.

"You gave this woman your cast-offs because you are old friends?" Hugh asked.

His voice filled the interior of the coach with strange vibrations. Or perhaps that was just Audrey's reaction to hearing it after they had been so long apart. She hadn't thought she would see him again. Half-hoped she wouldn't. Being in his company would only make *not* thinking of him more challenging.

"Of a sort," she replied, not ready to fully explain. However, she knew the Bow Street officer wouldn't stand for that.

"I'd like to hear how you and Delia are acquainted, and why the duke is not happy about it."

Philip sat up, more alert. "I never said as much."

"You did not need to."

Hugh was one of the most observant people she had ever met. Audrey could understand why Philip would chafe from such close inspection—she had been on the receiving end of

Hugh's scrutiny many times as well. There was no point in putting him off.

"I knew Delia some years ago," Audrey started off vaguely. "In September, I saw her in passing on Bond Street and invited her to Violet House for tea. Since then, we've met a few more times."

"How could you risk it?" Philip spluttered. "She is..."

"Of reduced circumstances?" Hugh offered, quickly puzzling out that she must have been, to have accepted Audrey's cast-offs.

The duke scoffed. "I am not so high in the instep to object to someone merely because of their financial circumstances, Marsden."

Hugh held Philip's stare, unflinching. "Then why?"

"Because of *where* she and my wife made their acquaintance in the first place," he answered, practically growling.

Long ago, Audrey had told her husband of her time at Shadewell Snatorium, an austere institution in northern England. She also told him of the few acquaintances she had made while there. Delia Montgomery had been one of them.

Philip deplored that Hugh also knew Audrey's deepest secret—that she had been committed to this asylum when she was but seventeen. Her mother and her uncle, Lord Edgerton, had arranged for the confinement after Audrey made the mistake of believing her gift—the ability to read the memories of objects and see into their immediate past—was something that made her special, and thus, something to share, at least with her family. But her mother, sister, and uncle had all been horrified, and off Audrey had been trundled to Northumberland for a two-year-stay to clear her "troubled" mind.

Hugh had vowed his confidence, and while Audrey trusted him, Philip was more skeptical. Probably because Hugh also knew of the *duke's* deepest secret. He wasn't comfortable with a

Bow Street officer knowing a truth about him that could lead to arrest, public humiliation, and quite possibly, execution. A forced stay at an insane asylum much like Shadewell could also be levied. Philip's first love—a young man he had met while at Cambridge—had suffered that last fate and ever since, Philip had feared exposure.

As the sixth Duke of Fournier, he had a responsibility to his title and family legacy, to maintain a strict level of respect and honor among his peers. The truth of his attraction to men would destroy not only him, but the Fournier name. Audrey understood his fear, and Philip matched hers with his understanding of why it was imperative no one find out about her time locked away at Shadewell. He did not discredit her for it, just as she did not discredit him for his feelings. She was quite certain that there were a number of men and women, even within their own social strata, that felt the same nonconforming desires. But they all lived within a fragile glass bubble, Audrey knew, where nothing was real or genuine, and the slightest crack could cause irreparable damage.

Hugh shifted his unyielding gaze, one that always felt like it was peering into her mind, from the duke to Audrey. "You met at the asylum."

Carrigan, their driver, called to the horses and brought the carriage to a halt. It introduced a drop of quiet into the brougham.

"We did," she said.

"There is no need to bring that up," Philip hissed, though she wasn't certain if he was speaking to her or to Hugh. "And you can stay here with Carrigan while Marsden shows me to the body. Have you not born witness to enough of them already?"

"While I trust Carrigan is a competent bodyguard, this is not a part of the city one wants to leave a woman alone in a carriage. The duchess will be safer inside the dead house with us," Hugh said, eliciting a glare from the duke and a half-grin from Audrey.

That one bit of mischief had breathed more life into her than anything she'd experienced in the last two months.

They stepped out into the damp and murky street alongside a nondescript brick and stone building. The briny stench of the river was strong here, as were more unsavory odors. Audrey removed a kerchief that Greer had doused with rose oil before deeming her suitable enough for a trip to what amounted to a mortuary. Her lady's maid had not made a single complaint when she entered Audrey's bedchamber in her nightrobe to help her mistress dress.

"Unidentified or unclaimed corpses are delivered here," Hugh explained as he entered the building and held the door open for Audrey. "If they are not claimed within a day or two, they're sent off for a pauper's burial. Unfortunately, some of the bodies are already in a state of decomposition when they arrive and so the smell can be challenging."

She gritted her molars and brought the kerchief to her nose and mouth. "That's putting it mildly."

"Oh, you should try visiting in the summer," he replied. Her stomach all but churned. The stale, rotting meat odor would have certainly been worse then.

They did not have to follow Hugh far to find bodies. They were on benches, tables, cots, and even the stone floor, covered by blankets and sheets. Makeshift shelving had been constructed within the winding passages, stacking three bodies at a time in places. Audrey was vigilant not to touch or brush against anything. She did not need any errant memories of these strangers' deaths to course into her mind.

Philip stayed adhered to her side while Hugh spoke to a bespectacled man wearing a soiled leather apron. Audrey didn't want to inspect the nature of the apron's stains for very long. Guttering lanterns lit the halls, and thankfully, cast many of the dead in shadow. If Delia was, in fact, the woman the patrolman had pulled from the river, Audrey hated to think of her here, among the unknown corpses. Delia had not been as fortunate as Audrey. Each time she came to Violet House, Audrey was reminded of that. And now, the stark contrast of their circumstances had reached an end.

"This way," Hugh said to them, then followed the attendant toward a table. Checking the tag strung around a bared toe, the attendant nodded.

"This here is the one," he announced, then unceremoniously pulled the sheet back to reveal a visage so hideously bloated and discolored, it did not resemble anything remotely like a face.

Philip swore under his breath, and Audrey barely had time to turn away before the grotesquely disfigured face seared into her brain. A second glance was not needed to know that identifying Delia in such a straightforward way would be impossible.

"I'd estimate she was in the water for at least a week," Hugh said, his voice calm.

"Aye, at least that," the attendant agreed. "The Runner what brought her in says she were caught up in fisherman's netting. Rolled up in a knot of buoys."

Audrey looked across the sheeted figure, avoiding the woman's still-exposed face, and admired Hugh's iron will. He had certainly seen many bloated corpses in his career and was no longer so adversely affected by the sight.

"How can we know if it is her?" Philip asked, his voice muffled. One of his handkerchiefs covered his nose and mouth as well. Even through the rose scent of her own, Audrey could trace the vile odor from the corpse. Her stomach churned. No one deserved this.

"May I see her gown?" Audrey asked, hoping for something else to gaze upon and tell her something informative. Hugh gave the attendant a nod.

The woman was not unclothed, or stripped to her under-garments, as bodies often were at death inquests. While Audrey had not been invited to the death inquest held for her late friend, Lady Charlotte Bainbury, she had let herself into the room prior to the inquest and had inspected her friend's belongings for any memories stored within them. Fabric was difficult to read; the energy they retained was usually weak, showing only hazy memories. But the dress Charlotte had been wearing at the time of her death had offered stronger images than usual, perhaps because of the circumstances. She had been chased through the woods and pushed from the edge of a quarry pit.

The attendant complied, pulling down the sheet further to reveal the gown on the body. Immediately, Audrey knew.

"It is Delia," she said, her voice soft. "I gave her that gown last month. Madam Gascoigne made it for me two seasons ago."

Hugh cut his eyes to her, a question lighting each dark brown iris. "Madam Gascoigne?"

"A modiste on Bond Street," she explained.

She had fallen in love with the silver satin, studded with hundreds of tiny, multifaceted crystals. Because wearing a ball gown more than once would be a fashion faux pas—one that could haunt a lady for years—Greer set Audrey's spent gowns aside, carefully wrapping and boxing each before putting them in storage. Every season, she and Greer went through them, determining which to give to charity, which to take apart and use for scrap material, and which Greer would like for herself. As she had always made it clear she did not wish for any evening gowns, only simpler morning dresses, promenade dresses, and day dresses for her days off, Audrey had been all too happy to see her most beautiful creations appreciated by Delia. A part of her had hoped she would sell the gowns to secondhand shops, as wearing them out would be impractical. But Delia had never quite seemed to care about practicality or convention.

"A modiste. Yes, of course," Hugh replied, then coughed before looking down at Delia again.

The water had ruined the satin. Sharp rocks, river detritus, and the abrasive hemp of the fisherman's nets had torn it in countless places. Strings of algae and river moss clung to the frayed embroidery, and dirt and sediment encrusted the fabric. As Audrey did not like to carry a reticule, she always had pockets sewn into the skirts, hidden by decorative tucks of material or embroidery. She didn't know why her card case would have still been in the pocket of this gown when it was given to Delia. Greer always cleaned and prepared her cast-offs with utmost efficiency. She could not imagine her lady's maid would have overlooked the case; it would have weighted down the skirts quite a bit.

As her eyes skipped over the spoilt and torn satin, a piece of cheap blue cambric stuck out of one such tear, as if it were a pocket turned out through the hole in the skirt. *Odd.* Audrey remembered this gown quite well, and there was no blue cambric lining, especially not of such low quality. She reached for the cambric, but then retracted her hand.

"What is it?" Hugh asked.

"The cambric," she explained, gesturing toward it. "It's an addition. Delia might have sewn in another pocket?"

The attendant eagerly reached for the cambric, but Hugh clamped a hand around the man's wrist. "I will see to that, thank you."

The attendant cleared his throat and stood back. Audrey

could only imagine the loot he and the other workers must have found within the pockets of the dead that came through here. Hugh turned the cambric out through the slit in the skirt; it looked to be an inner pouch, but it was sliced open, the pouch empty.

"She might have sewn money into the lining of the skirt," Hugh said.

"Gone now. Maybe it's why she were killed," the attendant suggested.

Audrey's stomach lurched, and she stared at the man, then Hugh. "She was killed?"

"Back of the skull's smashed," the attendant said with a shrug.

"Is that an injury that she could have sustained after she was already in the water, dead?" Philip asked, perhaps thinking of the many shipping vessels that plied the waters of the Thames. A strike from a keel could inflict damage.

"Nah, something hit her right here," the attendant said, pushing Delia's stiff body to the side, to indicate a back portion of her head. Audrey could not force herself to look. "If a boat or rudder had hit her, she'd have been torn up a lot more."

Hugh nodded to the attendant, who let Delia's body fall flat again, then pulled the sheet back up over the remains.

"How could no one have seen her for so many days?" Audrey asked. "At low tide, the pool of London is nothing but puddles."

Not that she visited the river very often to see it drain. In fact, she had not been to the Thames since last April when she had so foolishly gone to the docklands in search of Mr. Fellows's houseboat. She believed evidence of Philip's innocence in Miss Lovejoy's murder would be aboard, and she had found it—but Mr. Fellows had also found her. He'd shot her in the shoulder, and she'd taken a dunk in the stinking water. If not for Hugh's timely arrival and heroics in jumping in to save her, she would have drowned long before her untreated bullet wound could have killed her.

"At low tide, the detritus is everywhere," Hugh answered, then grimly added, "She would not have stood out among the rest."

"Heavy skirts like that would've anchored her right down," the attendant commented with an appraising nod.

"Your Grace, I am sorry for the loss of your friend," Hugh said. "Does she have any family I can contact?"

Audrey felt heavy as she shook her head, like a great weight was attempting to push her toward the dirty floor. Delia's family had washed their hands of her years ago when they had sent her to Shadewell. Like Audrey, Delia's family had arranged for her imprisonment. However, the circumstances had been far more appalling. Even thinking of them now made her shudder with revulsion.

"Any idea where she was living?" Hugh asked next.

"I..." Audrey glanced toward Philip and held her chin firm. "I think I might. A boarding house in Lambeth. Lark Street."

Philip swore. "Tell me you have not been in Lambeth."

It wasn't the finest part of London, but Audrey bristled at how much of a snob he sounded. "After our first meeting, I admit, I was skeptical. I don't believe in coincidences usually. So, I asked Carrigan to follow her."

When she'd spied Delia entering the boarding house, her stomach had twisted. The place was pitiable, and Audrey had felt guilty when she returned to her grand home on Curzon Street.

"Can you think of anyone who might have wished her harm?" Hugh asked.

"No, I'm afraid I was not privy to her...social dealings."

Delia's life in Lambeth could not have provided her with

much opportunity to frequent other, finer homes in town. Though, she had mentioned seeing another Shadewell patient, Mary Wood. Her real name, Delia had excitedly imparted, was Miss Mary *Simpson*—the false name of Wood shielded her identity while at Shadewell. Audrey had also employed a *nom de guerre* while there. Mary Simpson had only been a patient for a short time. She had been prone to violent fits of temper that could not be controlled, some of which would leave her in a frenzy of whole-body spasms. The few times Audrey had witnessed one of her episodes had been frightening. Would Delia have called on Mary, as she had Audrey? She then thought of it: the calling card case.

Earlier, at Violet House, she had not wanted to touch it when Hugh revealed it had been found on a corpse. But now, knowing it had been on Delia's person, and that she might have been killed, Audrey reconsidered. If she could hold it, read its memories, perhaps she could determine how her friend had found herself in this tragic situation.

She met Hugh's eyes. "May I have the card case now?"

His mind, sharp as a blade, caught her meaning immediately. He reached into the pocket of his greatcoat and extracted the case.

"No." Philip gripped Audrey's wrist to prevent her from reaching for it. "That will not be necessary, Marsden."

She pinned her lips against a grimace of annoyance. It was of no great surprise that Philip did not want her to read the object. After the conclusion of Lady Bainbury's murder investigation in August, he'd insisted they stay far afield of anything having to do with murder and scandal.

Upon their return to London, he and Audrey had discovered that society was clamoring for the whole story. The calls on Violet House and the invitations piling up in their salver would not cease until she assented, so Audrey accepted Lady Dutton's request for a stroll along Rotten Row. Considering the Viscountess Bleekeridge's reputation as a venerated gossip, she'd been assured one thorough telling of the investigation would inform all of society within a day. Ladies would no longer ask Audrey for the tale, but simply discuss it amongst themselves.

So long as no one showed the faintest interest in where Lady Cassandra Sinclair was, and why she was not participating in the Little Season, Audrey did not care what they said behind her back. However, she did care that the duke had spoken for her now, and that it had been so contrary to her own thoughts on the matter.

"I would like to take the card case," she said tightly, aware that the attendant was still present. He looked between Hugh and the duke, his eyebrows raised.

Hugh turned to the man, and with another nod of his head, dismissed him. The attendant seemed more than happy to return to his other duties. Once alone, Audrey lowered her voice. "Delia was killed, Philip. If I can help Mr. Marsden find something useful for his investigation—"

"It isn't my investigation," Hugh interjected. Audrey parted her lips, surprised.

"Who is in command of it, then?"

"No one. She was only brought to my attention because the patrolman believed it was you, and he was aware of our acquaintance."

An awkward moment passed in which Audrey was thankful she had not confessed to Philip about the near kiss at the quarry. He'd already told her that he sensed Hugh's interest in her but that the officer was "unsuitable" as a potential lover. The very idea of Hugh being her lover caused her cheeks to heat.

"But she's obviously been killed," Audrey said, hoping her blush would be mistaken for frustration.

Hugh took a wide look over his shoulder. "A number of these unclaimed dead were helped along into the afterlife, Your Grace. Bow Street simply cannot solve all the murders in London."

Audrey clenched her jaw. Why did it feel as though Hugh and Philip were teaming up against her? "Do you not want my help?"

Hugh's expression softened. A touch of regret, perhaps? "That is not what I meant. However, perhaps the duke has the right of it. Your involvement would not be proper."

Audrey hitched her chin, a dagger of hurt spearing her between the ribs. "You are suddenly concerned about *propriety*, Officer Marsden? After I've already helped you solve *five* murders?"

Hugh crossed his arms, and his eyes darkened another shade. "Those instances were also improper, and if you recall, my concern was well-founded. In both investigations, you were nearly killed." He exhaled, and then in afterthought, practically growled the appropriate, "*Your Grace.*"

"Why must you always toss that in my face?" she asked, her voice rising. "You've been in mortal danger a time or two as well, I'd wager."

He stepped forward, though the table holding Delia's body still separated them. "The difference is that *I* am a Bow Street officer, and *you* are a duchess."

"A duchess who has given you information that you would have otherwise never found on your own," she snapped back.

He parted his lips then sealed them again, his frustration causing the muscles along his well-formed jaw to jump.

"Audrey," Philip said, "Marsden is correct. Inserting yourself into another investigation when we barely came out of the last with our reputations intact would be unwise. Think of Cassandra. We don't need anyone whispering about us or asking questions."

The suppressed anger in Hugh's expression faltered. Wanting to stay angry, Audrey cut her gaze from his before she could see any sliver of care in his eyes. Hugh knew the truth about Philip's sister: she had been taken advantage of by Lord Renfry, ruined thoroughly, and was now in Stockholm with trusted friends of Philip's until after the birth of her illegitimate child. It was yet another secret Hugh had been trusted with, and as much as he was currently agitating her, Audrey still did not doubt he would keep their confidences.

Cassie's reputation would be destroyed should the truth emerge, and she and Philip had agreed that maintaining a low profile was instrumental in deflecting curious gossipers. *We need to be thoroughly dull, my darling,* he'd told her in September upon their return to London. Since then, the pair of them had been just that.

She took a deep breath and exhaled. "Please at least assure me that Delia's death will be investigated, officer."

Hugh winced, and she wondered if it was in reaction to her cold, detached tone.

"I will look into it," he said. For a moment it appeared as though he wanted to say more, but then he cleared his throat and stepped away from the table.

Audrey peered at the sheeted figure of her Shadewell acquaintance one last time, and then turned on her heel. Tears brimmed in her eyes as she made a hasty exit from the dead house. The emotion wasn't just for Delia, but for the knowledge that her ability—the very one she'd thought might make her useful to Hugh and Bow Street—was being rejected once again.

~

THE NEXT MORNING, Greer entered Audrey's bedchamber after her single, pert, telltale knock. She'd thoughtfully waited until nine o'clock, an hour later than usual, to enter the bedchamber and rouse the duchess. Audrey had not been able to sleep anyway and had been languishing in bed since dawn.

"This came for you, Your Grace," Greer said after opening the drapes and allowing in the milky morning light. Audrey sat up in bed, her head aching from lack of sleep, and peered at the small, brown paper-wrapped parcel as Greer set it into her waiting palm.

"Officer Marsden's smelly urchin came to the servant's entrance with it," Greer said, wrinkling her nose. "Mrs. Comstock says he charmed her into giving him a link of sausage too."

Instantly, Audrey knew what the nondescript box held. Her heart fluttered as she pulled the twine bundling the parcel. The paper fell away, revealing her silver card case. A message had been scrawled on a scrap of paper, tucked underneath the case:

Find me afterward.

THREE

Hugh arrived at Delia Montgomery's boarding house early the next morning. Lark Street was like most of the streets in Lambeth: narrow, busy, and poor. This was a corner of London he had unfortunately been to countless times to arrest all sorts of unsavories. That the Duchess of Fournier had been acquaintances with a woman who resided here, had brought her in for tea, and passed along her fine clothing to her, continued to puzzle him. Their shared experience at Shadewell must have bonded them on some level, though Miss Montgomery's reasons for being there had to have been vastly different than Audrey's.

Sleep had been impossible when he'd returned to Bedford Street. Frissons of relief still worked their way through his limbs whenever he recalled seeing Audrey on the stairs at Violet House, alive. Still, the fact that she had known the murdered woman clung to his mind like a thorn. How was it that she could have a connection to yet another murder victim? Was she cursed? Was it somehow linked to her unnatural ability to read objects?

As he stood outside the boarding house, his hands in his

pockets, Hugh felt the clump of calling card stock between his fingers. He'd removed the ruined cards from the silver case earlier that morning. The duchess would not be needing them, but the case *was* her property, and it was only right that he return it. If the case showed her something that could help provide information on the poor woman lying in the bone house, all the better. While considering the potential benefits and pitfalls of involving Audrey any further, Hugh had absent-mindedly picked at the stack of card stock. Peeling them apart, one by one, he'd found something unexpected: they did not all belong to the Duchess of Fournier.

He'd made up his mind and had sent the case off with Sir, whom Hugh had found in his kitchen breaking his fast. Mrs. Peets had taken to having toast and two hardboiled eggs ready for the lad come eight o'clock. If he was polite, she brought out the jar of marmalade. If he was surly, she made him wash his own dish afterward. That morning, he'd pocketed the second hardboiled egg and strutted off with the parcel for delivery to Violet House. *Make sure it gets to the duchess—not the duke,* he'd instructed, and Sir had winked theatrically.

Hugh had agreed with Fournier that Audrey should not involve herself. He'd resolved to investigate as thoroughly as he could and send a note to the duke and duchess, informing them of his findings. Contacting Audrey would be improper, and after the quarry pit ledges, even the slightest hint of familiarity would be disastrous.

And yet, he'd paced his study, then lain abed, wide awake, unable to get her hurt expression out of his mind. If he had never learned the truth about her mother and uncle sending her off to an asylum, treating her as though she was not only a freak of nature, but worthless enough to abandon for two years, Hugh might have been able to brush off that wounded look, or the glassy hint of tears pricking her deep blue eyes before she'd averted them. Though she wore a near impenetrable mask of indifference, their treatment of her had injured her thoroughly. Lastingly. Hugh could not endure the thought that he might have as well.

And when he'd seen the other cards among her own, he'd known Audrey had more information to give.

Hugh brought his fist down upon the door to the boarding house. A woman appeared after a few moments, a skeptical glint flattening her eyes.

"What d'you want?"

"Miss Delia Montgomery."

The woman pulled her worn shawl over her plain gray dress as she stood within the threshold. "She ain't here."

Behind her, the entrance hall to the home was dark and drab, with yellowed paper on the walls and little adornment.

"When did you last see her?" he asked.

"A week or so, I'd guess. Why? Who're you?"

"Principal Officer Marsden from Bow Street."

The woman pressed her lips thinly. "What sort of trouble did Delia get herself into now?"

"Is she apt to find herself in trouble?" he asked, intrigued by her question.

She pulled the shawl tighter. "Nothing too terrible. Though, some fancy gowns she turned herself out in lately made me suspect she pinched them."

If Delia had worn Audrey's cast-off ballgowns here, she would certainly have stood out.

"This your establishment?" he asked.

She wiggled her shoulders a bit, something he'd witnessed many people do when they were preparing to tell a falsehood. "It is. Name's Mrs. Roy."

The emphasis she placed on "Mrs." let Hugh know she was not, in fact, married. Most housekeepers and landladies advertised themselves as married for propriety's sake. It didn't necessarily mean this woman was not to be trusted, but he would tread carefully.

"Does Miss Montgomery share her room with another boarder?"

True boarding houses often double or triple stacked each room, but instinct told him that this house might have been a bit different than a run-of-the-mill lodging place. It wasn't uncommon for women to use rooms to sell themselves and for landladies to act as madams. Prostitution was not illegal, of course, and though there was a ban on keeping a brothel, Bow Street did not arrest women for it. Molly houses, on the other hand, were a different story. Just last year, a molly house had been raided and the men within it arrested and pilloried. Beyond that incident, a handful of men had been hung for gross indecency as well. It was unfair, but Hugh didn't make the rules.

"She did—Winnie—but I let the room to another when Delia cleared out her things and took off." The woman jerked her chin. "What is this about, Runner?"

"Is Winnie here?" Hugh pressed.

"No. Now either tell me what Delia's done or shove off." She grabbed the door, as though intending to slam it in his face.

"Miss Montgomery is dead, and I want to know how she came to be that way."

He watched the woman's reaction, waiting for something to clue him in to guilt. But she reacted appropriately: lips parting, facial muscles going slack, eyes softening at the corners.

"Oh," she said, blinking as if to absorb the news. "What happened to her?"

"She was found in the river. A blow to the head."

The woman's cheeks paled. Hugh wanted to take advantage of her shock and continued, "I'd like to talk to Winnie."

Mrs. Roy snapped to attention. "I already said she wasn't here."

"And if I were willing to pay for her time? Would she be at home then?"

The woman's eyes flashed. Then tempered. "I don't want no trouble from Bow Street—"

"Your business doesn't interest me. All I want is to speak to Winnie and see what she can tell me about Delia."

Mrs. Roy, still looking suspicious, nodded. She allowed Hugh inside and led him into a shabby sitting room. "Wait here," she said, and then exited.

Hugh took in the room. Though clean, the rug was aged with scorch holes near the hearth, and the furnishings were mismatched and threadbare. He did not have to wait very long before the landlady returned with a young woman at her side. She had dark brown skin and curly hair, and she wore a dress that revealed a generous figure. Her eyes were wide and fearful.

"You are Winnie?" he asked.

She nodded, then darted a hesitant look toward Mrs. Roy, who held out her palm. "A shilling. Up front."

Had Sir asked for his payment up front, Hugh would have told him to peel off. But the rules were different in a brothel. He palmed the coins in his pocket, next to the waterlogged calling cards, and handed them over.

Winnie waited until Mrs. Roy had stepped out before she spoke. "Is it true? Delia is dead?"

Hugh nodded, and the young woman stared around the room, gaping in shock.

"Were you close?"

She sat limply on the arm of a sofa. "We roomed together two years."

He wasn't certain that was an answer but decided to leave it for now.

"What can you tell me? Had Delia been seeing anyone? Any regulars who might've given her trouble?"

Winnie shook her head. "No. She had a few regulars, but they were all nice enough. One bloke brought her a hand pie every time he came 'round." She smiled, thinking of it.

"Why did she clear out her things? Did she say where she was going?"

Winnie's smile dropped. "She didn't say nothing to me about it. I came back from the dance hall one night and her things were all gone. No goodbye, nothing. She's gone off before, a week here and there. But she'd never taken her things."

The timing of her hasty departure from her lodgings and her death suited. Had she been running from someone?

Winnie continued, "I knew she didn't much trust me, but I thought she liked me a little. At least enough to say so long."

"Why didn't she trust you?" he asked.

"She thought she was being sly about it, but I knew she was sewing her money into the linings of those fancy dresses she kept getting. Didn't trust me not to steal it."

That explained the cambric pouch Audrey pointed out at the bone house.

"Fancy dresses?" he repeated, pulling on that loose thread to see what more Winnie might know.

She snorted. "Aye. Said an old friend had started giving 'em to her. I dunno. I think she might have nicked 'em."

As Mrs. Roy had thought as well. And why shouldn't either of them think that? Delia had been a prostitute. Poor, with little opportunity. She had been killed and pushed into the river. While reprehensible, it wasn't exceptional. The women who lived their lives this way, whether they wished to or not, were perpetually at risk. But the card case, and the different cards he'd found among Audrey's was one route he wanted to follow.

"Do the names Simpson, Rumsford, or Fournier mean anything to you?"

Winnie scowled. "Should they?"

"Delia never mentioned a Mrs. Simpson? A Lady Rumsford or Lord Fournier?"

She shook her head again. "Sorry."

He was getting nowhere. Hugh sighed heavily. "Don't apologize. Thank you for speaking with me."

Winnie stood from the arm of the sofa, her expression changing. She lowered her lashes and pouted her lips. Hugh had been in plenty of establishments of ill repute to know that particular look.

"A shilling's worth at least another half hour, and Mrs. Roy said I was to be extra nice to you."

The woman was likely worried that Hugh had lied and was going to report her after all. Winnie brought down the shoulder of her dress, but Hugh held up his hand. "That isn't necessary. You've been very kind. I'll take my leave."

Winnie covered her shoulder and gave another careless shrug, likely relieved by the rejection.

"If you remember anything more," Hugh said as he found another sixpence in his pocket, and then pressed it into her palm, "send word to me at Bow Street."

She stared at the coins before quickly slipping them into her bodice, where Mrs. Roy would never find them or take her gouging cut. Winnie nodded and thanked him, but he already knew she had nothing more to offer.

Outside, he took the calling cards from his pocket. The paper had bloated then dried, and the inks had distorted, but the pressed letters had mostly remained legible. He flipped through. There were at least three apiece for the Viscountess Rumsford, Mrs. Gregory Simpson, and the Duke of Fournier. Hugh spent a protracted moment eyeing the duke's card. Block engraving with no flourish beyond the family crest stamped in the top center. Why would Delia have his calling cards, and who were the owners of these other two?

While the duke's calling cards intrigued him the most, he had no desire to see Fournier—or the duchess—so soon after their outing the night before. Greeting a viscountess before the more acceptable one o'clock in the afternoon also did not appeal.

He would visit Mrs. Gregory Simpson first, he decided, and see what she could tell him about the pitiable Delia Montgomery.

FOUR

Audrey settled herself into the silk cushioned chair inside Mrs. Gregory Simpson's receiving room and forced an awkward smile. Mrs. Simpson had been breathless ever since her maid announced Her Grace, the Duchess of Fournier just moments before Audrey entered the room.

The older woman's flushed cheeks and wide, agonized eyes were likely the result of having been called upon by an elevated lady of society. Audrey did not enjoy the stiffening of postures, the hitching of chins, and the demure smiles that greeted her whenever she was presented formally, but it could not be helped. Surely, when she woke that morning, this middle-class woman had no notion that a duchess would visit her residence.

"*You* are the Duchess of Fournier?" Mrs. Simpson's tone was not one of shock, but of doubt. And now suddenly, the breathless, wide-eyed stare struck Audrey as hostile rather than surprised.

"I am," Audrey replied, curious at the woman's blatant doubt.

After a moment in which Mrs. Simpson appraised the duchess, she nodded to the maid. "Tell Mary she may come back in."

Audrey frowned, following the maid's departure with gaping lips. Apparently, she had sent her daughter from the room before Audrey had been shown in. As the woman called for tea and apologized for her qualms, Audrey puzzled over why she'd been so suspicious. And when Mary joined them, the young woman's eyes widened so perilously, they nearly rolled out of her head. Her coloring pinked, then paled. Audrey sent her a stilted grin, and for a second time, extended her apologies for not sending a note ahead. Mrs. Simpson waved the apology away with a bright laugh, insisting such notice was not necessary.

"Why, we are honored to host you, Your Grace, are we not, Mary?" She sent her daughter a fierce look of expectation.

Mary, who was perhaps twenty now, quickly stifled her surprise and changed her expression to one of perfect graciousness, even though her coloring continued to alternate between stark white and a mottled flush. "Yes, of course, Mama."

The blank, beseeching look Mrs. Simpson turned upon Audrey next needed no interpretation. She wished to know why the duchess was currently ensconced within her receiving room.

"I am not sure how to begin," Audrey said, crossing another glance with Mary, who once again appeared ashen. "Mrs. Simpson your daughter and I are already acquainted. We met several years ago in Northumberland."

This was a gamble, and it was one Audrey was willing to make if it meant learning more about Delia's brutal end. As she'd suspected, the silver card case had shown her nothing more than murky, distorted images when she had attempted to read its memories. It was as though any energy the object had retained had been watered down by the Thames itself. So, with no clues to go on, she had settled on beginning with Delia's previous mention of Mary Simpson.

Her mother now stared in dismay, eyes swiveling from Mary to Audrey and then back again.

"What? Surely not. North...*Northumberland?*" Her voice pitched high and breathy, and Mary's trained poise fled. She slouched, her forehead creased with dismay, and her jaw slackened.

"Yes. A certain *retreat,*" Audrey said, referring to Shadewell as her own mother always had when describing the place. The baroness had never once acknowledged that it was an asylum. Audrey suspected that was to protect herself from feeling an ounce of guilt—or more likely shame—over sending her daughter there.

Mrs. Simpson glared at Audrey and went utterly still as if she had been transformed into stone. "So, you *do* have some connection to that woman."

Audrey frowned. "What woman do you mean?"

Mrs. Simpson's chin tightened, her lips thinned, and she again peered at the duchess as if she were an enemy.

"Mother," Mary said softly. "Connection to whom?"

"Your Grace, I am afraid you are misinformed. My daughter has not been to a retreat of any sort."

"*Mother,*" Mary said again, this time more insistent. "There is no use in pretending. The duchess is quite aware."

"Mrs. Simpson, I mean you no harm," Audrey said quickly. "I have kept my own past with this retreat confidential, and I have no intention of sharing Mary's stay there any more than *you* plan to share mine. Do I have that right?"

She held the woman's direct stare as the meaning of her sentence sunk in. She hadn't known what kind of woman Mary

Simpson's mother would be. A vapid gossip or a conniving one? Either could ruin Audrey, should the woman start whispering about the duchess's unexpected call and what they had discussed. But she'd been willing to wager that Mrs. Simpson would do anything to keep her daughter's stay at Shadewell secret, including promising the duchess her confidence. If she breathed one word of gossip about Audrey, her own daughter would suffer the same, if not greater, ruin.

Mrs. Simpson stiffened her spine, her eyes falling flat with loathing. "I do not know what your intentions could possibly be, but I will *not* be blackmailed again."

Stunned, Audrey began to speak, but the maid returned with the tea service, and the three ladies were made to sit quietly while the tray was delivered. Mrs. Simpson dismissed the maid curtly, and only when the room was theirs again, did Audrey continue. "You won't be blackmailed *again*? Do you mean to say someone has blackmailed you before?"

The woman huffed mirthless laughter. "As if you are unaware! Today is not the first time someone has gained entry to my home by bearing *your* card."

Hot confusion swarmed Audrey as her mind reached for an explanation, and yet failed to grasp anything before the maid appeared within the threshold yet again.

"Mrs. Simpson, you've another caller. A gentleman who says he's with Bow Street."

The lady went bleakly pale. Mary did as well. Audrey, however, felt only impressed awe. How in the world had Hugh found his way to the Simpson household? She hadn't once mentioned Mary Simpson to him! The only information she'd given him was the location of Delia's boarding house. Which meant he must have found something there to bring him this way.

As he entered the receiving room, Audrey took a sip of

piping hot assam. Her eyes met his over the gold-tipped brim of the cup.

He tensed one corner of his mouth; an expression that said her presence was not wholly shocking.

"Your Grace," he said with a bob of his head before turning to the lady of house. "Mrs. Simpson, I presume."

She sprang to her feet. "What is this about, Runner?"

Audrey cringed. Like most Bow Street officers and patrolmen, Hugh was not fond of being called "Runner." He preferred his ranking to be used, the same as titled lords and ladies did.

"My name is Officer Marsden, and I've some questions for you about a woman named Delia Montgomery." His eyes shifted toward Audrey. He likely suspected she'd already launched into her investigative questions.

"Delia?" Mary echoed, and then turned her confounded gaze to Audrey. "Is that why you've come as well?"

"I'm afraid so," she replied.

"Unfortunately, I must report that Miss Montgomery has been found dead," Hugh said quickly, as though wanting to beat Audrey to informing them. She suppressed the urge to reproach him with a glare.

"What? No!" Mary's coloring drained even further from her cheeks. "That is...that is awful. What happened to her?"

A deep pleat formed between Mrs. Simpson's brows. "Who is Miss Montgomery? How do you know her, Mary?"

Hugh stepped forward, his hat under his arm. "I would like to know how *you* knew her, Mrs. Simpson." From his waistcoat pocket, he withdrew a slim rectangular card. He extended it to her. Mrs. Simpson's hand went to her throat as she accepted it.

"A few of these were found among her belongings," he explained. "I'd like to know why."

Audrey craned her neck, trying to see what he had handed

over, while Mary stared at her mother, slack jawed. "That's your calling card, Mama! *You* visited Delia? But...how? You don't even know her."

Mrs. Simpson pivoted on her heel and went toward a draped window, the card fluttering to the carpet as she dropped it.

Hugh and Audrey exchanged another thoughtful glance, his brow hitching. He then looked pointedly toward Mary. Audrey cleared her throat, understanding his silent request for an introduction.

"Officer Marsden, may I introduce Miss Mary Simpson," she said, and the young woman, her eyes shining with tears, sniffled as she made a polite curtsey.

Then, because it would hamper their discussion much less if everyone was on the same foot, Audrey continued boldly, "Mr. Marsden is aware of my stay at Shadewell. He has vowed his silence, and he will vow the same for you, Mary. Isn't that right, Mr. Marsden?"

"Of course," he said without hesitation, even though he could not have known Mary, too, had been at the asylum. He masked his ignorance well, even as Mary and Mrs. Simpson whirled to stare at him, then Audrey.

"How dare you?" Mrs. Simpson hissed. "Your Grace, you have no right!"

"On the contrary, Mrs. Simpson, the duchess is only saving us from a prolonged and complicated conversation. Delia Montgomery also stayed at Shadewell, which answers how the duchess and your daughter are connected to her. However, it does not answer why your cards were amongst her things."

Mrs. Simpson pinned her lips, her fury stifled for the moment. "Very well. I...I think she may have been the young woman who was blackmailing me."

Audrey set down her tea, answers unspooling in her head. "Delia presented *my* card to your maid when she called on you. That's what you meant when you said it had been used to gain entry to this home before."

Mrs. Simpson arched her brow. It seemed her suspicion of Audrey had been well founded. She had likely believed Delia had come again—only to be met with the real Duchess of Fournier this time.

"She was threatening to reveal your daughter's stay at Shadewell, I take it?" Hugh asked.

"Yes, unless I paid her a handsome sum." The woman scoffed at the ultimatum. "She never told me her name, only that she was a collector for some anonymous person who knew Mary had gone to Shadewell for... Well, it doesn't matter does it?"

Hugh assured her that no, it did not matter why Mary had been sent away. Audrey knew, of course. Doctor Warwick, the superintendent at Shadewell, had called Mary's fits of temper symptoms of "hysteria." Attempts to calm her had only made her worse. Laudanum was the only thing that had worked. After a handful of months of tranquility, Mary—no more than fourteen or so at the time—had been sent home. Audrey vividly recalled her own feelings of envy every time a patient would be released. She had started to doubt she would ever be one of them.

"With Mary still unwed, I could not risk ignoring the demands and possibly damaging her prospects. And now, with her upcoming betrothal announcement..." Mrs. Simpson fought what might have been a swoon. She sat back onto the sofa without much grace.

"My felicitations, Mary," Audrey said to the young woman, whose distress partially lifted to be replaced with a smile of delight.

"The banns will be posted next week," Mary said, her eyes bright. "Mr. Burrows is a clerk at the Home Office."

"Mr. Simpson's protégé," Mrs. Simpson put in with obvious pride. But then her doughy chin trembled. "It is a very good match indeed."

One she did not want to risk for her daughter, to be sure.

"No, it's not possible, Mama. Delia would never blackmail you." Mary's shining eyes now filled with earnest tears. They slipped down her reddened cheeks. "She never even said a word about calling upon you."

Mrs. Simpson gawked. "How—? When did *you* see her?"

Mary swiped at her cheeks. "The last time was just a few weeks ago. I couldn't tell you—I knew you would never allow it, but you don't understand, Mama. Delia was not as fortunate as I. Or Her Grace," she added with a wobbly grin in Audrey's direction.

Before Mrs. Simpson could splutter more questions, Audrey jumped in. "How was it that you and Delia became reacquainted?"

As Mary haltingly explained that she and Delia had run into each other by chance in late August, Audrey began to form a suspicion, however tentative and flimsy.

"I admit, I did not recognize her at first," Mary said. "She appeared so different from how she looked at Shade—"

Her mother hissed through her teeth, and Mary went silent, lips pinning together tightly.

"I ran into Delia a few months ago by chance as well," Audrey said, catching Hugh's eye. Wasn't it a bit odd for Delia, after a handful of years, to have encountered two of her former acquaintances by chance?

"How often did you see her?" Hugh asked.

"Sporadically." Mary glanced tentatively at her mother, as if preparing for censure. "We would meet for ices or tea usually. After that first time, she was always dressed so nicely..."

In the cast-offs Audrey had given her, most likely. But to have mentioned the state of her appearance twice now, as if it was in defense of Delia, made Audrey wonder if perhaps Mary knew the truth about Delia's most recent circumstances. She had been living in a boarding house in Lambeth, but the few comments Delia made over the course of their meetings led Audrey to believe she was entertaining men for coin. Of course, Delia had not come out and confessed it—she claimed to work in a milliner shop off Oxford Street.

"The last time you saw her," Hugh began. "Was there anything different about her? Did she say anything strange or unusual?"

Mary shook her head. "No. Nothing. She just spoke of her work as a milliner's assistant and how she was about to move into a new set of rooms."

"Mary, how could you?" her mother interjected, pacing away from the window and back toward the sofa, her fingers twisting together in dismay. "To be seen with someone who could connect you to that place—I had no idea. You should have told me!"

Mary shot to her feet. "And you should have told me about Delia's calls. Does Papa know?"

Mrs. Simpson tucked her chin and blanched. "Gracious, no. He has no earthly idea, and I couldn't say anything to him—or to you—even if I'd wanted to. I was warned against it."

"Miss Montgomery warned you on behalf of the blackmailer?" Hugh asked. "Or is it possible she was the blackmailer herself?"

The woman snorted her disbelief. "The letters I received asking for increasingly larger amounts were well written, the penmanship fine. *She*, however, sounded like a fishmonger's wife."

At Shadewell, Delia's use of cockney had been uncouth at times, her manner unrefined. Once at Violet House, when Audrey offered to give her a few books from her library, Delia had laughed and asked what she'd do with them.

"You still have not explained why Miss Montgomery had your calling cards," Hugh reminded her.

Mrs. Simpson sighed wearily. "It was part of the instructions. When that woman came to collect, I would give my calling card to her along with the sum. It was rather burdensome collecting the money, considering Mr. Simpson did not know, but I managed it."

Audrey wondered how the card would benefit the blackmailer—unless Delia and the blackmailer were using the cards to gain entry to homes, as they had with Mrs. Simpson. A caller might leave their card with the footman or maid; other times, they took their card back. To have a supply of cards would not be unwise for Delia and the blackmailer. Audrey shook her head. Like Mary, she still could not believe that Delia would be part of such a scheme. She had seemed simpleminded, not conniving.

"Perhaps now that the woman is dead the letters will cease," Mrs. Simpson stated coldly. Audrey clenched her teeth against a reprimand and saw Hugh grimace.

"If you receive another, I ask that you let me know," he said. "I do not believe you are the only one Miss Montgomery or this anonymous person was blackmailing."

Mrs. Simpson agreed, though it was half-hearted, and Audrey was almost certain that should another letter arrive, she would handle it as she had the others: pay the sum to protect her daughter, at least until after she was married to Mr. Burrows.

Feeling as though she had entered the receiving room and utterly upended the mother's and daughter's lives, Audrey stood to take her leave. Hugh joined her.

"You were supposed to find me and let me know what the card case showed you," he said softly as he tugged on his hat and stepped onto the walk along Chancery Lane. The early November air was brisk and uncharacteristically sunny.

"I would have, had it shown me anything other than the color brown." Audrey considered holding back, but then, in a moment of charity, added, "Thank you for delivering it."

He gave a nonchalant shrug as if it was not important, but his lips suppressed a smug grin.

"How did you make it here before I did?" he asked as Carrigan opened the door to Audrey's carriage. He and Hugh exchanged pleasant greetings, and Audrey recalled that the Bow Street officer had marked respect for her driver-cum-bodyguard.

"I must have risen earlier in the day," she replied.

"Very funny."

She smothered a grin then turned earnest. "Delia mentioned she'd seen Mary and where she lived. I figured you would visit Lambeth and I could visit Holborn."

She'd briefly considered going to Lambeth but had known that to go there during the day would be too public and to go at night, too dangerous. Even here, near Russell Square, Audrey avoided making eye contact with those passing by and hoped she would not be noticed by any of the men or women currently slowing their gaits to observe her and Hugh as they spoke near her open carriage. It was more than unseemly to be in conversation on the curb like this.

"Can I give you a lift to Bow Street, Mr. Marsden?" she asked. Only after making her offer, did she consider that they would be alone in the carriage.

He scratched at his chin, which was freshly shaved, and glanced over his shoulder at the passersby. "Rumors might fly."

"That tends to happen regardless of what we do or don't do," she said, then before she could change her mind, climbed into the carriage. She was hopeful he would accept, if only so that they could discuss the revelations Mary and Mrs. Simpson had delivered. That they would be alone was of no consequence, and she was determined not to act awkwardly.

Hugh joined her, and Carrigan shut the door. They started away from the Simpson's doorstep but didn't speak for a few moments as they joined traffic. Long enough to make Audrey wonder if this had been a mistake after all.

"Do you know the Viscountess Rumsford?" Hugh asked just as Audrey broke the silence with, "Delia stole my calling card case."

They both went still and silent. Hugh smiled and gestured to her to speak first.

"Greer is far too efficient to have left my case in the pocket of a gown I planned to give away. Which leads me to think she must have somehow stolen it." That Delia would sneak into her study, where the case and calling cards were kept in a desk drawer and steal them made Audrey's stomach twist. Why would she befriend Audrey but blackmail Mary?

"It seems likely," he replied. "It appears she was a collector of cards. Mrs. Simpson's was not the only one I found."

"Viscountess Rumsford, you said?" Audrey shook her head. A viscountess... *Oh.* "I think I might know of her. We aren't acquainted, though my sister might be."

Millie, the Viscountess Redding, moved in a different circle of peers than Audrey and Philip, and that was not something either sister lamented. They were as different from each other as Audrey was to her mother and uncle, though that could have been exacerbated by their difference in age. She was nearly ten years Audrey's senior. Audrey had been much closer to James, her late elder brother. But then, she'd only been seven when he'd died. How close could they have really been, what with James away at Eton at the time?

Hugh took another card from his waistcoat and handed it to her. Lady Rumsford's card was without a single flourish. A bold line engraved the space directly beneath her name.

"She seems a very straightforward woman, if her card represents her correctly," she said, handing it back. Hugh tapped the corner against his thigh. Audrey dragged her eye away from the sand-colored buckskin. "I'll call on her," she said.

"You will not." He tucked the card away again. "You've already gone against the duke's command—"

"No one commands me, Mr. Marsden."

A spate of temper filled her at that word. Husbands had legal privilege to rule their wives as they saw fit, but Audrey could not conceive such a marriage—the kind she would have been made to endure had she married the Earl of Bainbury, as she nearly had. She and Philip had laid down rules for their marriage, which would have been deemed radical by anyone else. Commanding each other in any way, shape, or form was strictly forbidden.

Hugh paused, assessing her for a moment. Perhaps even rethinking his approach. But he surprised her when he said softly, "We all live under the command of someone or something, Your Grace."

She could not argue against that. Though he was working class now, he had not always been. He knew as well as she did how difficult it would be to thwart the peerage. Even in his role at Bow Street, Hugh lived under the command of a higher-up: Sir Gabriel Poston, the chief magistrate.

"Your marriage might be unconventional, duchess, but I

sensed strong frustration in the duke last night. His patience is not without its limits."

Yet again, she wished Hugh were not so observant. Most people could not, or did not, bother to look beneath the veneer of the façade she and Philip had perfected over the last few years—that theirs was a completely content love match. They might not fawn over each other in public, but their union was obviously warm and gratifying for them both. The only thing that would make their marriage more perfect would be the addition of a child. An heir to the Fournier dukedom.

Audrey averted her eyes from Hugh's unwavering stare. "It's Cassandra," she said, startling herself with the truth. He knew about her situation, and it was no great surprise to find herself content in being able to speak to him about it.

"How is she?" He truly wanted to know; she could tell by the changed tone of his voice.

"She is staying on with Philip's friends in Sweden. Her letters describe a rather boring existence, but it's the best we could do for her, given the circumstances."

Meanwhile, Lord Renfry, the baby's scoundrel of a father, had already secured another betrothal, after the dissolution of the previous one. That lady had learned the truth about her fiancé's wretched seductions of his stepmothers and had cried off.

"I'm surprised Renfry didn't come to the duke, asking for Cassandra's hand after he lost out on the rich merchant's daughter," Hugh said. Audrey pinned her lips, delighting in the memory of the day the blackguard actually had done as much.

Hugh read her expression and leaned forward. "No. Tell me he did not."

"Oh, he did."

He barked a laugh and slapped his thigh, then sat back against the cushions. "Did the duke plant him a facer?"

"If he had not, I would have," Audrey said, chuckling. "Renfry left with a bloodied lip and the threat of a bullet to the heart if he ever so much as set one foot near Cassie again."

And she had no doubt Philip would follow through. His younger sister had been completely manipulated and deceived, all for Renfry's own sport. The man deserved to be called out. However, to make his transgressions public would only lead to requiring Cassie and Renfry to wed, and neither Audrey, Philip, nor Cassie wanted to be linked to such an immoral cad.

"But he does not know about the baby?" Hugh asked, once again with concern. He did not know Cassandra well, but he seemed to take an interest. The barest twinge of envy pricked at her insides. Surely, he did not care for Philip's sister in a romantic manner. Although, she *was* young and pretty...and unmarried.

Then again, it had not been Cassie whom Hugh had been a breath away from kissing on that quarry ledge.

No. Do not think of it. She inhaled and answered his question. "He doesn't know, and he will not know. When the baby is born..."

She sealed her lips. It wouldn't be right or proper to tell Hugh what Philip had proposed—that Audrey feign a confinement, travel to Sweden, and return with the child as if it were her own.

Cassie had refused the proposal, as had Audrey. Philip, however, had argued in its defense. They would have an heir. The gossip about her barren state would subside. And Cassie would be able to see her child grow. But Cassandra had claimed it would be unbearable to see the child but not mother it, and Audrey had agreed. She would never feel like the child's true mother. It was already difficult enough not feeling like a true wife.

"It must be a difficult situation for her," Hugh said after a few silent moments.

"You are more understanding than others would be."

"I have experienced something quite similar," he replied with a wry lift of his brow.

Ah. So that was why he took an interest; his own mother had been in Cassandra's position at one point, although Audrey did not believe the Viscount Neatham had treated her as Renfry treated Cassie. From everything she had heard about the late viscount, he had been a good and decent man. To raise his illegitimate son among his legitimate children and care for Hugh's mother did him credit.

"So, you see, things have just been strained lately. We're a bit unsettled," she said.

Returning to London, keeping up the façade about Cassie forgoing the Little Season to nurse her great aunt back to health in Scotland, and to recover from the shocking murders at Fournier Downs over the summer, and then of course, beginning to repair their own reputation after the scandal in April. Sometimes, there seemed to be too many obstacles to overcome.

Hugh sat quietly as the carriage rattled toward Bow Street. Then, just as the silence was beginning to elicit a strange friction in the air, he spoke. "Have you told the duke?"

She knew without hesitation or confusion what Hugh meant by the question. Audrey shook her head. "No," she said softly.

"I was inappropriate. You are within your rights to—

"Don't be absurd. I have not told the duke anything because there is nothing to tell. You did not kiss me." Heat flooded her almost instantaneously. Why had she used that word?

"What would he do if I had?"

She tensed her brow, the air in the carriage turning hot. "How do you mean?"

"Would he call me out?" He was not acting flippant or playful. His questions were as direct as they had been when he'd been questioning Mrs. Simpson.

"Call you out? Of course not," she answered, but then considered. "Although he might be angry. He does not think you are suitable."

As soon as she spoke, she wished she had not. Hugh's rich brown eyes narrowed. "Not suitable for what?"

Her cheeks warmed. "Let's not speak of it, please. It doesn't matter anyhow. Nothing ...happened." Though only because they had been interrupted.

She expected him to continue pressing for an answer if only to tease her, and perhaps if they had not arrived at the Bow Street offices, he would have. She would have undoubtedly given in and explained that the duke had warned that the officer could never be a suitable lover for a duchess. Until Philip had given that warning, she had not even allowed herself to imagine that Hugh *could* be her lover. She and Philip had agreed from the outset that they would each allow the other to associate outside the normal confines of a marriage—if they discussed it first. Philip had already broken that promise and had seen another man, Lord St. John, secretly. He'd apologized profusely, and Audrey had forgiven him. But she had no plans to go behind Philip's back. And though she hated to even think it, a Bow Street officer *would* be an unsuitable prospect for a duchess's lover.

Hugh exhaled and nodded stiffly, clearly not happy to relent. "Very well."

She paused, waiting for him to provide a caveat. But he only sat forward and opened the door, beating Carrigan to the task.

"Thank you for the lift. And *I* will call on Lady Rumsford, Your Grace."

His order was clear—she was not to involve herself again.

Audrey inclined her head as he jumped down to the pavements outside number four Bow Street and adjusted the collar of his coat against the new drizzle of autumn rain. She said nothing, refusing to verbally agree. Carrigan shut the door on Hugh's scowl. He knew her game: She would call on the viscountess with or without his permission.

CHAPTER
FIVE

T he woman's shrill laughter was beginning to grate on Hugh's last nerve. He clenched his back teeth and raised the snifter of whisky to his lips as Thornton attempted to lift his voice above the incessant giggling. They were settled in Thornton's sitting room after the dinner he'd hosted for his brother's birthday celebration. Not Lawrence, the heir to the Lindstrom marquessate, or Harold, the spare.

"They are far too important to attend such a lowly celebration," Thornton had joked when Hugh inquired if they would make an appearance. No, the revelry was for the third son of the Marquess of Lindstrom, James. Thornton, the fourth son, was closest to James and hosted a birthday rout every year for his favorite brother. The house on St James's Square would be packed to the cornices with everyone from *demimonde* to working class. Artists and actors, courtesans, merchants, landed gentry, and maybe even a noble or two.

Hugh looked forward to the bash every November, however tonight, he had a difficult time relaxing. A longing to excuse himself and return to his own residence was oddly intense. The din of conversation—and that blasted woman's laughter—was agitating him more so than usual.

He blamed it entirely upon the Duchess of Fournier.

He wished to god he hadn't said anything to her about the intimate moment they'd shared back in Hertfordshire. The flush of her cheeks had only made him want to leap across the carriage and kiss her properly this time. Being alone with her again had tied a knot in the base of his stomach, and without her needing to confess it, Hugh knew she had been trying to avoid speaking of the incident. He should have matched her effort.

For the rest of the day, he'd had trouble focusing on the investigation into Delia Montgomery's murder. To make things more complicated, Sir Gabriel had been skeptical of Hugh taking on the investigation.

"She might have bashed her skull when jumping into the river for all we know," he'd said, throwing up his hands. "The woman was a prostitute. She has no family, no one at all to give a damn about her death. Why are you so keen on this?"

To mention the duchess would have only inspired questions from the chief magistrate. He'd not only demand to know how Audrey knew the dead woman, but he'd bring up the all too evident fact that once again, Hugh was involving himself with the Duchess of Fournier. He'd vowed to keep Audrey's history at Shadewell a secret, and he would go to his bloody grave with it. Protecting her from any questioning, any doubt, any harm, burned like a fire in the very center of his soul.

"Did you hear me, Marsden?"

Thornton's voice cut through his thoughts. Hugh swallowed his whisky and focused on his friend, although he was unable to confirm that he had, in fact, heard him.

"I'm having trouble hearing anything beyond that baying,"

he murmured, inspiring a few knowing grins from the two other men he and Thornton were standing with.

"It's not like you to be so uncharitable, Marsden," one of the men, Mr. Jefferies, said, though his smirk indicated his comment was all in good humor. Mr. Jefferies stiffened as the source of the baying laughter trained her attention upon their small circle. He and the rest of them straightened their postures as she cut toward them, a glass of wine in hand.

"And why so many sullen faces in this corner?" Miss Martha Devereaux asked as she joined them. As a popular member of the demimonde, Miss Devereaux maintained a reputation that would have scandalized the ladies of the peerage. It did not matter that she maintained close relations with various lords of the *ton*—she was not "quality" and she reveled in it. Not all women wished to be of peerage ilk. In fact, Hugh could see why the looser, less restrictive numbers of London's "half-world" usually appeared more content.

"If we seem sullen, it is only because we've been left out of your revelry, Miss Devereaux," Thornton replied, employing the charm that tended to net him an over-abundance of female company.

Hugh could not fault his friend for it; after losing his beloved wife and infant daughter in childbirth several years ago, Thornton had succumbed to a dark place. He'd been lost to the world, including to Hugh, for a long time. He'd crawled out of his lonely abyss of grief eventually, but he had no intention of marrying again. Instead, he accepted the comforts of women like Martha Devereaux. No ties. No requirements. No expectations.

It was not very unlike Hugh's arrangement with Gloria, although he didn't imagine Miss Devereaux restricted her liaisons to just with Lord Thornton. At the thought of Gloria, Hugh waited to feel the longing for her company, as he once used to. Before, waiting all week to see her had built up a need within him, and lately, their increased meetings had been a fire unable to be extinguished, kindling just underneath his skin. However, though he waited for the tightening in his groin and the clench of desire, it eluded him.

Miss Devereaux batted her lashes but did not direct her favor on Thornton. Much to Hugh's annoyance, the woman settled her hand on his own shoulder.

"Why, Lord Thornton, I am afraid I see through to the truth of the matter," she said, her voice unnecessarily loud. "Your Bow Street friend hasn't so much as grinned once this evening. He is far too serious for a celebration."

Hugh sipped his whisky. "The lady is not wrong."

"Of course, I am not," she simpered, draping herself more closely. "Tell me, officer, is there any truth to the rumors I've heard?"

He peered at her, her face much too close to his own. "Rumors rarely involve truth. However, I'm curious as to what you've heard."

Miss Devereaux leaned heavily on his arm; her perfume drifted into his senses, and he waited, yet again, to feel the taut reaction of lust in his groin. It did not arrive.

"Oh, just that a certain duchess has taken an interest in your *investigations*," she said playfully running a finger along his shoulder. "And that she has her duke in quite a cuckhold."

Hugh went utterly still.

Thornton did as well, pausing his whisky halfway to his lips. "*Martha*," he hissed.

Hugh shrugged off the woman's hand. His temper rose to a sudden boil as he took a step away from her. "I suggest you think twice before perpetuating such gossip in the future. Your cheap amusements could have unfair consequences for finer women, such as this duchess you speak of."

The lash of his tongue and the insult leveled left the circle of men and Miss Devereaux gaping. Hugh sliced his irritated stare toward Thornton, who was already apologizing with a shame-faced expression, and stepped away from them.

"Hugh, wait." Thornton followed him through the pockets of guests toward the front hall.

"I don't know if I should be flattered or disturbed that your post-coitus chats with Miss Devereaux include me and the duchess," Hugh said as he accepted another whisky from a foot-man, whose cheek sported a smudge of vermillion lip paint, and whose neck had been draped in a rope of pearls.

Thornton snagged Hugh's arm before he could leave the room.

"I'm sorry. I slipped up just after the duke's exoneration," Thornton said, attempting to tone down their conversation for the rest of the crowd. Thankfully, James was holding many of the guests in his thrall as he told an exuberant and no doubt exaggerated tale of hunting a pair of bucks in Essex.

"I'd had too much brandy, and she was asking about you and the duke. I suppose I revealed too much about the duchess's actions during the investigation."

It was so rare to see his friend utterly chagrinned that Hugh had a hard time staying angry with him.

"Did you say anything about the duchess being shot?" he whispered.

Thornton shook his head. "No. I promise, I did not."

Hugh exhaled, grateful. Audrey had not wanted anyone to know about the injury, as the knowledge that she had been attacked at the Thames on a houseboat by a murderer would have been just another grave blow to her and the duke's already tattered reputation.

That didn't mean he was not still peeved. "You need to find yourself a better mistress," Hugh grumbled.

Thornton widened his eyes and cocked his head. "Does Miss Hanson have anyone she would recommend?"

His mention of Gloria did the opposite of what Hugh would have liked; he felt a ball of dread weigh down his stomach. Much like when Audrey had mentioned Madam Gascoigne at the bone house. Gloria had once told him the modiste created a few of Audrey's gowns, but the knowledge had since slipped his mind. That Gloria had likely helped create the duchess's gowns was a link between the two women he did not need or want.

"Don't press your luck, Thornton."

He only laughed, and Hugh settled for calling him a prick. Thornton was the closest thing he had to a brother, and thankfully, he didn't piss him off very often.

"Tell me what you know of Lord Rumsford," Hugh asked, intending to change the course of the conversation. He did not want to discuss Gloria or Audrey or anything at all having to do with mistresses. Work was a much more palatable topic.

"Rumsford?" Thornton pulled a face. "Why?"

It was only the smallest of twitches, but Hugh still saw it upon Thornton's expression. Like he'd just met with a mind-twisting riddle.

"You do know him then?" Hugh asked.

"I do," he said tentatively. Cautiously. "What is this about? Fournier?"

Hugh lowered his whisky glass and the rest of the conversation in the room muted underneath his renewed focus. "Why would you suggest the duke?"

Thornton, though taller than Hugh, seemed to shrink at being snared. He'd given something away and shook his head, knowing it.

"All right. You've got me. If I can trust that this will go nowhere but between us?"

Hugh beamed at him with obvious sarcasm. "I cannot promise Miss Hanson will not hear of it."

"Devil take you," he groaned. "Lord Rumsford and the duke are…" He thought for a moment, then finished, "likeminded in their tastes."

Hugh grappled with what that meant until the widening of Thornton's eyes pushed him toward understanding. His friend, having been present when Hugh and Audrey had confronted and overwhelmed Lord Wimbly, the mastermind behind last April's scandal, knew of Fournier's preference for men. He'd vowed his confidence, and Hugh trusted him.

"How do you know this?" Hugh asked. Thornton grinned and looked around the room.

"Do you not see my acquaintances, Marsden? The demimonde is welcoming to all, and Rumsford is not as shrewd as the duke," Thornton said quietly, turning his back again to the rest of the crowd, including to Miss Devereaux who watched them with a hawk's interest.

"Others know about Rumsford's activities?"

Thornton nodded. "Some do. He's also rumored to have left London for a length of time. A few years ago, if I recall. Some hushed up business after a molly house raid. Sarah mentioned his absence after attending a luncheon with Lady Rumsford."

Thornton did not often speak of his late wife. That he brought himself to do so now proved to Hugh the length to which he was willing to go to make amends for blabbing to Miss Devereaux.

Hugh didn't ask where the viscount was rumored to have gone. He was almost certain he knew—Shadewell was likely to be a place for men as well as women. The connection between Delia, Mary Simpson, Audrey and now Lord Rumsford was becoming too solid to consider mere happenstance.

Shortly after Audrey delivered him back to Bow Street, Hugh

had traveled to the address engraved upon Lady Rumsford's card. He'd made sure to arrive before the fashionable hour when the viscountess might be strolling along Rotten Row, but the footman had turned him away with the excuse that the lady was out. For a brief moment, he'd wished the duchess had been with him to help ease his way into the lady's drawing room, much like she had done in August when visiting the Marquess and Marchioness of Finborough to speak to them about the so-called suicide of their daughter. But then, Hugh had felt immediately guilty for the wish. Audrey's card had been used in such a manner by Delia Montgomery, and there he was, thinking of using the duchess herself in much the same way.

"What about Rumsford has you in a twist?" Thornton asked.

"He or his wife is connected to the death of a woman, though I'm not sure how," Hugh said. His admission would be safe. Thornton might have been loose-lipped before with Miss Devereaux, but he would not make the same misstep again.

"What woman?"

Hugh shrugged a shoulder. "No one of great import, though I should be struck down for saying it. A life is a life. Still, she had no family, was no one of consequence. Hell, she had only some fine dresses cast off to her and a few other worldly possessions. Sir Gabriel doesn't think I should spend time investigating. Give her a pauper's funeral and let it be. Move on to bigger fish."

"But?" Thornton crossed his arms in expectation.

Hugh sighed. "But I cannot."

Thornton quirked the corner of his lips into a wry grin. "Tell me what the duchess has to do with this."

Irritation spiraled through him, reminding him of why he should not keep friends so close. "Who said she had anything to do with it?"

"You would not defy the magistrate otherwise. And considering your outburst back there regarding the duchess, I'm convinced you've seen her recently."

Hugh glared at him, but he did not back down. More than once before, Thornton had made some comment about Hugh's troublesome interest in the Duchess of Fournier. It had been easy to brush off, at first. But after the case in Hertfordshire, he was willing to admit his friend might have seen something Hugh himself had not.

He relented, and in a hushed voice, explained to Thornton all that occurred from the time Constable Stevens brought him Audrey's drenched card case and Mrs. Simpson admitted to being blackmailed by the deceased—all but Audrey's own involvement at Shadewell. Instead, he said Delia was a charity case that the duchess took on. A relation to one of her house staff. He didn't like lying to his closest friend, but it could not be avoided. Once Hugh concluded, Thornton's expression was contrite.

"I don't think I'd be able to walk away from that muddle either," he admitted. And then, the pale green of his eyes darkening, added, "You think Rumsford is also being blackmailed?"

Hugh suspected that to be the case. But then, he had also found the duke's calling card among Delia's things. It was possible she'd stolen those alongside Audrey's when she'd somehow managed to go snooping through Violet House. However, Hugh wondered if there wasn't another reason.

"I was turned away today when I called on Rumsford," he admitted. Thornton snorted a laugh, unsurprised. He scratched his chin and considered.

"I could accompany you," he suggested.

"I would rather do this on my own." Not just for his pride either. He would need to speak of Shadewell, and the topic of the duchess might rise to the surface. As much as he valued and trusted Thornton, he could not betray Audrey.

"Let me send a request, at the least," he insisted. "A note to recommend you."

Hugh nodded, appreciating the offer, and yet also hating that he needed such a favor. Not for the first time, he wondered what life might have held in store for him had he not been called out by Viscount Neatham, the younger. Five years later, hatred for his half-brother continued to simmer. Not just for Bartholomew either. Thomas and Eloisa had been complicit in Hugh's ruination. Even thinking about them turned his stomach. At least he had left Barty with a physical reminder of just how much he despised him.

"My lord." Goodwin, the butler at Thornton House, slipped up beside them like a whisper. "Mr. Marsden's malodorous wretch is in the kitchen, demanding to see him."

Hugh stifled a grin and asked Goodwin to bring his coat and hat. He would not be returning to the festivities. He bid Thornton a goodnight before going to the kitchen, where he found Sir sitting on a tall stool next to a wash basin, gnawing on a leg of roasted chicken.

"I thought I told you to meet me at Bedford Street," Hugh said.

With his mouth full, a speck of chicken meat on his upper lip, and grease shining on his chin, the boy replied, "But Mrs. Dort cooks here, and her cooking's worlds better than anything Mrs. Peets makes."

"That isn't polite now, young man," Thornton's cook chided, but Hugh also caught a sparkle of pride in her eyes at the compliment. She was soft on the boy, just like every other motherly type, including his own cook Mrs. Peets. Hugh supposed it was his skinny legs and arms, and his emaciated torso that made every cook want to heap food onto him.

"Sir—"

"I kept my blinkers on the duchess, just as you asked," he

said before Hugh could chastise him. "Went to that address, like you said she would."

Hugh had expected nothing less after he'd asked Audrey not to call on Lady Rumford.

"And?" he pressed.

"Got snubbed," Sir replied.

He should not have relished the strike of victory as much as he did. Of course, no doubt Audrey would attempt to call on the viscountess again tomorrow. Hopefully, Thornton's recommendation would allow Hugh in first.

"You're also snooping around that boarding house like I've asked?"

Sir made an assenting sort of nod and grunt as he chewed off more meat. Hugh anticipated having to wait for the lad to lick the bone clean before he got any answers.

"A bunch of blokes come and go from that place," he said after another hefty swallow. "The drowned lady met with some regulars."

From where she stood at the stove, Mrs. Dort gasped and glared at them. Hugh sent her an apologetic grin and stepped closer to Sir before lowering his voice. "Any names?"

"Teddy, Ivan, and Beaver."

"Beaver?"

"On account as he always wore a top hat," Sir answered readily, finally finishing off all but the gristle. "But the landlady isn't up to much more than shouting at her boarders most of the time."

The names of Delia's regulars might not prove useful, but Hugh had wanted to have a pair of eyes on the place, on the off-chance Mrs. Roy had been holding back anything at all about her dealings with Delia Montgomery, or if anyone had come around asking about her. But Sir shook his head and said it was all just business. Nothing had caught Sir's attention, and the boy was astute.

"All right then, you can quit boarding house duty."

Sir tossed the chicken leg bone into the kitchen sink basin, and from Mrs. Dort's look of exasperation, Hugh figured it was not supposed to go there.

"You sure, guv? It ain't so bad, you know. Those ladies've taken a real shine to me. Winnie especially."

Goodwin appeared with Hugh's coat and hat, and Hugh bit back a laugh as he accepted them. He could easily imagine the women at the boarding house cooing over the lad, and Sir soaking up the adoration.

Hugh tossed him a shilling. "Of that, Sir, I have no doubt."

CHAPTER

SIX

Audrey knew someone would eventually snub her for the scandal involving Philip last spring, but she had not expected it to sting so fiercely.

She had been sitting within the brougham outside the Viscountess Rumsford's home while her footman presented one of Philip's cards at the door. Her own card had caused distress and suspicion at Mrs. Simpson's home, and Audrey did not want to take the chance that it would be received the same way here. If Delia was in possession of the viscountess's card, there was a strong chance she had been blackmailing her the same way she had been Mary's mother. So, she'd stealthily taken one of Philip's, which he kept in the top left desk drawer in his study.

However, after a few impatient minutes of waiting, her slippered foot tapping the floor of the carriage, the viscountess's solemn-faced footman reappeared in the doorway and handed the card back to Audrey's servant. The door then closed again, and the footman returned to the carriage.

"It seems her ladyship is out, Your Grace," he said shortly before climbing back up onto the driver's seat next to Carrigan.

Audrey's foot stilled, and shame flooded her chest and cheeks. She'd brought Greer with her, and the lady's maid said nothing as Carrigan started back toward Violet House.

The viscountess was indeed at home—her footman would not have disappeared for nearly five minutes had she not been. No, the viscountess had seen it was the Duke of Fournier calling on her and had decided to give him the cut. Refusing to invite in a caller was the ultimate statement of rejection. And if Lady Rumsford's servants were anything at all like the rest of the serving class of the ton, the *on dit* would begin to make its way around London's finest addresses without ado. Though she and Greer rode back to Curzon Street in silence, over the next several hours, her embarrassment transformed to something she was much more familiar with—determination.

By late the next morning, her second plan to speak to Lady Rumsford was well into formation when a message delivered to Violet House threatened to upend it. Miss Mary Simpson had sent word ahead, announcing that she would be calling on the duchess at four o'clock to discuss something "pertinent" to their previous conversation. Audrey folded the note with a groan and lamented the poor timing. She would not be at home to receive Mary, as she would be busy attempting to speak to Lady Rumsford. As intrigued as she was to know what Mary wanted to say, the viscountess's involvement with Delia was still unknown, which sparked Audrey's interest more. She'd sent a reply stating that six o'clock might be a better time and then prepared for her afternoon outing.

Though it was now November, and the sun was setting earlier with each passing day, the many paths through Hyde Park continued to be a center of activity for the fashionable set in the late afternoon. The wide corridor of the King's Private Road, better known as Rotten Row, traveled past the Serpentine

River, and it was by far the most popular spot to see and be seen.

Just before four o'clock, curious gazes fell upon Audrey as she languidly strolled the footpath along the water, her lady's maid a few steps behind. She met with polite smiles and greetings, but no one stopped her for a proper hello. Had she wished for such interaction, she might have been disappointed. However, socializing had never been among Audrey's assets. She had been raised the same way every other lady of the peerage had been, taught to care about the same things, and strive for the same distinguishments. And yet, she had never quite been able to ignore the preposterousness of it all. The insignificance of it. Did no one else see how trivial their lives were? How little they were actually *doing*? Audrey had often pondered that thought, and the more she explored it, the further away she felt from everyone around her. Especially among women who were truly comfortable with their positions in society.

For those reasons, being seen in Hyde Park could not have appealed to Audrey less. But as she forced a starched grin and a well-bred greeting toward a pair of ladies who had crossed the path in front of her to purposefully catch the duchess's eye, she reminded herself of why she was here.

Greer had gotten it from Charlie, the under butler at Violet House, who had gotten it from his cousin, a groom for Lord Yancey, who just so happened to be Lord and Lady Rumsford's neighbor, that the viscountess almost always quit her house at four o'clock to take a constitutional stroll through Hyde Park. So, near to that time, Audrey and Greer had set out once again for King Street and waited a little way down for the viscountess to step out her front door and be whisked away in her carriage.

Snubbing someone from the privacy of one's drawing room was one thing; giving the cut direct in full view of society while on Rotten Row was another level of seriousness altogether. Audrey was risking much; should the viscountess turn up her nose, there would be no end to the gossip. But it seemed a silly thing to worry about—hadn't there been a deluge of gossip regarding the duke and duchess since April anyhow? She wasn't in the practice of giving up, and if Delia's involvement in some blackmailing scheme had gotten her killed, Lady Rumsford might have critical information.

Of course, Hugh Marsden might have already visited Lady Rumsford's home and gleaned all that the woman knew. Audrey had not heard from him, and nor did she expect to. Yesterday in the carriage, when he'd brought up their near kiss, Audrey had been all too aware of her own reaction—the memory so visceral and immediate, it might have only been a single day since he'd clutched her to him and bent his head toward hers.

But what of *his* reaction? He'd seemed much more guarded and solemn. Repentant. Perhaps he regretted the impulse so thoroughly that he felt none of the same strange friction under his skin that she did when thoughts of him crossed her mind. Now that he was aware that the duke did not know, and even if he did, would not call him out, it was possible Hugh Marsden wished to put the mistake behind him.

He would be right to, of course. It was the best course of action. Perhaps Hugh was only better at dismissing something as simple as a close embrace because he had done so many times in the past. He had surely been involved with other women in a more serious nature.

Audrey had only a few moments to question why the notion weighed so heavily in her stomach before she heard Greer cough politely behind her. The duchess broke from her troublesome reverie and quickly found the viscountess ahead on the path. Opportunity was upon her.

A few steps behind Lady Rumsford, a pair of footmen trailed with a matched set of small, white, long-furred dogs. Each footman held a leash and were carefully pacing the dogs so that they trotted alongside the viscountess, one on either side of her.

"Lady Rumsford," Audrey said as the woman approached on the path. She deplored the knob of anticipation in the center of her throat, the slight fluttering of her pulse, and the desperate hope that when she drew to a stop, the viscountess would as well.

Lady Rumsford, a matronly woman in her fourth decade with an austere mien, eyed Audrey skeptically, her attention taking in every last thread and detail of her appearance from the tips of Audrey's walking boots to the crown of her emerald velvet bonnet, adorned with a wide black silk ribbon.

"Forgive me, it's been some time since Lady Redding introduced us," Audrey fibbed. In truth, Millie had never done so. "I am Audrey Sinclair, Duchess of Fournier."

The woman's reaction was just as violent as expected. Flaring nostrils and rounded eyes preceded a swift look around to see if there was any chance of her escaping without a scene. The pair of dogs ruined her chances. The footmen leading them lost their dignified control and crossed leashes, causing the pups to yip and bounce about excitedly, drawing attention their way.

"Your Grace, of course," the viscountess said loudly, and then stepped closer to her, away from her boisterous dogs. She wasted no time lowering her tone and adding, "This is no coincidence, is it? I knew that could not be the duke calling on me yesterday. What are you playing at, Your Grace?"

"And how would you have known such a thing?"

"I *suspected* it," she amended, her discontent masked by another false grin as a lady and gentleman ambled past them. "I have never met the duke and *your* card had been presented before."

So, it was true. Audrey drew in a breath, both victorious and incensed. Delia had employed her ruse with Lady Rumsford as well. She had sullied Audrey's name with Mrs. Simpson and the viscountess, and who knew how many other people?

"A young woman presented it?" Audrey asked, to be certain.

"What is your connection to her?" the viscountess snapped.

Audrey had anticipated such a question and had a story at the ready. "She was the daughter of a longtime employee at Violet House."

The lady narrowed her shrewd eyes. "Was?"

"She is dead," Audrey revealed.

The viscountess hitched a brow. "Good. I do not care if it is a coarse statement. I've never been prone to sentimentality anyhow."

Audrey bit back an instant retort that Delia had not deserved to die, no matter what she had done. But the truth was, she didn't quite know everything Delia *had* done. It would better serve her to stay focused on why she'd tracked the viscountess down and cornered her. It's what Hugh would have done. Even with all the bewildering feelings she had for him, she at least knew and respected his questioning tactics.

"She was blackmailing you?" But then, thinking of Mrs. Simpson's situation, she amended with, "Perhaps about a relative of yours? Someone you care for?"

Lady Rumsford peered back at her dogs and footmen, then jutted her chin, a signal for Audrey to fall into step beside her. They walked a glacial pace along the path. "How do you know this? The woman claimed you weren't involved, even though I had my doubts after that scandalbroth last spring."

Ignoring the mention of Philip's arrest, Audrey asked, "How long had Miss Montgomery been paying you calls?"

"*Montgomery*," she snorted. "Was that the chit's name? Your servant must have done something considerably wrong to have raised a daughter who would dare extort money from a peer."

The woman had a right to her bitterness. Had Audrey not known Delia, she would have readily agreed. However, she had known her. So had Mary Simpson.

"How did you know her?" she asked Lady Rumsford.

"*I?*" she replied, aghast. "I did not know her at all."

"But she knew something about you," Audrey pressed.

"What are you about?" the viscountess asked again. "How are you involved in all this?"

"She was murdered. My servant wants to know what sort of trouble their daughter was wrapped up in," she lied, yet again. It was becoming entirely too easy. How often did Hugh lie, she wondered, to get the answers he sought?

"What use could that be for your servant now?" she retorted, and Audrey had to admit, she was right. But she could not let the viscountess wiggle her way out of an answer.

"You were not the only one being blackmailed. Another woman I have met was paying Miss Montgomery a large sum of money to keep a secret about her daughter from being fed to the scandal sheets."

Delia, Mary, and Audrey were all connected to Shadewell. What were the chances Lady Rumsford's loved one was as well? To ask was a great risk. Mrs. Simpson's position in society would not allow her to cross the duchess, and though the viscountess was lower than Audrey in social rank, she was a formidable and shrewd woman.

"What secret?" Lady Rumsford asked.

"I shouldn't say. But she would not have been able to weather the scandal of it, had it been made known."

She huffed. "Neither would the viscount."

It was her husband, then. *Lord Rumsford*. Audrey did not know a single thing about him.

"You were instructed to keep him ignorant of the blackmailing?" she presumed. The viscountess confirmed it with a solemn nod. "And to give one of your calling cards?"

Lady Rumsford again peered at Audrey with barely concealed mistrust. "I didn't understand why, but yes."

Delia must have used that card to her advantage. To gain entry into yet another fine home in London, perhaps.

They strolled in silence for a few more moments before Lady Rumsford blurted out, "You are sullying yourself dealing with these matters, Your Grace. Or is it that you've grown bored with the duke and have taken an interest in that Bow Street ruffian I have heard so much about as of late?"

Audrey's feet tripped to a halt. The mention of Hugh Marsden seemed so misplaced and unbidden that she could only stare incomprehensively at the viscountess. This was the first gossip she had heard yet hinting at her connection to Officer Marsden.

The viscountess's lips turned up as she realized she'd hit her target. "Don't tell me that disgraced by-blow has charmed you into believing you can be of use to him? How provincial."

Audrey nearly clapped back with the argument that Hugh wasn't a disgraced by-blow but bit her tongue. He *had* been born on the other side of the blanket, and even he had admitted it. That Lady Rumsford had seen through to the truth of the matter—that Audrey had started to feel useful in these investigations—made her feel uncomfortably transparent.

"There is more to me than just my title, Lady Rumsford," she said, though she hated giving the woman's taunting even an inch of acknowledgment.

"Perhaps there is," the viscountess said. "However, your title is the only thing that has kept London society from sweeping you out the door. If the blackmailer is dead, then there is nothing more to be said on the matter. I will ask you not to approach me again. Good afternoon, Your Grace."

Shame nearly drowned her as she watched Lady Rumsford's stout figure walking away, her footmen and dogs following, the latter yipping happily. No one of rank had dared speak to her so bluntly since Philip's scandal. While she'd feared their top-ranking status had been the one thing keeping them from being totally shunned, hearing it from the viscountess—a woman she did not even know—had felt like being plunged underwater and held there to splutter and flail while her chest burned for oxygen.

Again, Greer let out a dainty cough. Audrey blinked, coming back to attention, and immediately moved toward where Carrigan waited with the carriage. The flames on her face had cooled slightly when the driver met her with a wrinkled brow.

"You've a visitor within the conveyance, Your Grace," he said, looking as though he'd sucked a lemon.

"*In* the carriage?" Audrey echoed.

"He wouldn't allow me to deliver the message, and I couldn't have him standing about, considering..." He opened the door. "I didn't think you'd object, Your Grace."

Her olfactory senses certainly did. Her nose traced him before her eyes did. As Carrigan handed her into the carriage, she touched the tip of her nose to block the odor of onions, manure, and unwashed hair and clothes. "Gracious, Sir," she said, coming to sit across from the boy. He laid on his back, lengthwise across the bench, arms crossed behind his head.

Greer had smartly remained outside with Carrigan. Audrey lowered her hand and forced herself not to comment on his dire need to bathe. "Why have you refused to give my driver your message? He is more than trustworthy."

"Mister Hugh always says I got to deliver his messages

m'self," he replied, springing up from the bench. "Says I'm to fetch you."

Her heart gave an involuntary stammer. Lady Rumsford's comment, however, clung like a briar, and she tamed her pulse. "For what purpose?"

The boy sat forward, his pale cheeks streaked with dirt and a smear of what appeared to be jam. "There's been a murder."

Alarm strummed through her, and Audrey sat taller. "Do you know who it is?"

He nodded and grimaced. "A girl named Miss Mary Simpson."

CHAPTER SEVEN

H ugh paced the carpeted lobby outside Mary Simpson's bedchamber. He had his arms crossed, his eyes skipping to the clock at the top of the stairs on every pass. A footman stood there, one of the scant few Mr. and Mrs. Simpson employed. Their home was modest, their staff numbering a half-dozen, and all wore the shock of the afternoon's grim discovery upon their faces.

At just around two, a messenger had come to Bow Street with an urgent request for Officer Marsden to hasten to High Holborn. He'd recognized the address.

"A woman is dead," the messenger, young and scrawny like Sir, yet not half as fragrant, had said, huffing for air.

With his stomach quickly turning to lead, Hugh had set out for the Simpson household. There, he'd found Mr. Simpson, a clerk with the Home Office, attempting to console his insensible wife, while also succumbing to moments of incomprehension. Not unaccustomed to such moments of grief, Hugh turned to the maid who'd seen him into the house the other day—and who'd had the clear-headedness to send for him at Bow Street —and asked her to explain.

Less than an hour before, the cook had found Mary Simpson's body on the steps of the servant's entrance. Her throat had been slashed. When Hugh had started toward the kitchen and the back entrance, the maid had hurried to say the young woman had been taken upstairs and lain upon her bed.

"Why?" Hugh asked, trying to temper his fury at the handling of the body.

"Mrs. Simpson insisted," the maid answered, grimacing. "She couldn't leave Miss Mary out on the steps like that."

He'd swallowed his frustration. It wasn't the maid's fault, and nor had Mrs. Simpson meant any harm. She and Mr. Simpson had lost their child. Their only child, from what Hugh quickly learned, and he could only imagine the toll it would take on them. He'd seen fathers of dead children expire from heart failure, and grieving mothers screaming for someone to kill them so they could join their child in the afterlife.

After inspecting the steps and shouting at the footman to stop scrubbing the blood from the stones, Hugh had gone up to view Mary's body. She had been tucked into bed with a sheet lain out over her. Her eyelids were pressed closed, her hands folded over her chest. As if she had merely been sleeping. Only the dark slash of her throat and the blood soaking the neck and bodice of her gown had revealed the grim truth. The maid insisted no one had washed her, and a quick look at her hands and nails showed no signs that Mary had attempted to ward off her attacker.

After questioning the staff as to what they knew, and then attempting to also question Mr. and Mrs. Simpson—without success—Hugh had gone outback, behind the kitchen, for a breath of air. Sir was waiting there, a ready and willing assistant. How the lad found him and how he knew just when to appear continued to impress him.

"What d'you need, Mister Hugh?"

With the connection to Shadewell shared by the two dead women hanging over his head like a damned guillotine, and because of something Mary's maid had imparted, he'd had only one need in mind: "Fetch the duchess, Sir. Bring her here. To me."

Now, he waited in the upstairs hallway, the house feeling isolated from the rest of London. Death was odd like that. One person stops breathing, their life snuffed out, and yet millions of others continue with business as usual. Life was relentless and pitiless, and nothing illuminated that more than a recently dead corpse.

Sound broke through the muffled house as the front door opened and soft murmuring traveled up the stairwell. Even in whispers, his ears knew her voice.

Hugh met her at the top of the stairs, her blue eyes round with disbelief, the apples of her cheeks, normally pink, now pallid. "Tell me Sir was wrong."

He shook his head and stepped aside for her join him on the landing. Audrey grasped the newel post.

"How?"

"A knife to the throat," he replied. The footman nearby flinched, and Hugh drew Audrey away, lowering his voice. "She was on the servant's entrance steps when she was attacked. No one saw or heard anything. The maid claims Mary was preparing to go out on a social call."

"Oh, good Lord." Audrey closed her eyes. "She was coming to see me, at Violet House."

"For what reason?"

Audrey shook her head, still holding onto the newel post as if it was the only thing keeping her upright. "Her note said she had something pertinent to discuss regarding Delia and the blackmailing, but she didn't write specifics." She paused and drew in a deep breath. "Do you think whoever did this wanted to stop her from speaking to me?"

"It's possible," he replied. In fact, he thought it most likely. He only wished he knew what Mary had wanted to say to the duchess. Something that she had not been willing to say the other day when in the company of her mother, or something she had learned since then?

"Mrs. Simpson..." Audrey murmured. "Does she know anything?"

"She can barely string two coherent words together."

She nodded, blinking and shaking her head at the same time. "She was to be married..." Her voice caught and trembled. "Where is she?"

After sending Sir off with his task, he had tried to think of a way to deflect the duchess's certain desire to view the body. She was not afraid to set eyes upon the dead, that much he knew. Hell, she'd once broken into a death inquest.

"They laid her out in her bed. But I cannot allow you in."

She peered at him, a strange fire lighting her eyes. The tremulous emotion of sadness flashed over to irritation. "Why on earth not? I have seen dead bodies before."

He gritted his teeth, wishing to hell he'd found a good enough reason to keep her out of Miss Simpson's room. It wasn't the murder scene, after all, and so unfortunately, the best excuse he had was that it would be unseemly. Audrey was sure to bark laughter if he attempted to say that. The duchess was long past caring whether she appeared unseemly. And there was no one about but the servants anyhow.

Hugh gave in and shoved open the door closest to them. The coming evening light had dimmed Mary's bedchamber to a putty gray. The drapes had been drawn all afternoon and now, shadows drenched the room.

Audrey stepped inside, her attention landing directly upon the bedstead. Mary's figure lay there, a single thick plait of dark hair standing out against the white pillow. The bodice of her dress was soaked with blood, darker crimson now that it had dried some.

"The attack on her is no coincidence, is it?" Audrey whispered.

"No." He watched her as she approached the side of the bed. Any other woman of the peerage would have likely dissolved into a fit of the vapors, but Audrey had an uncanny steel spine when she needed it. Hugh had seen her vulnerable side too, on more than one occasion. In those moments, he'd wanted only to whisk her into his arms and protect her from harm. Yet moments like this, he admired her strength.

"Poor Mary," she said, moving from the bedside toward the window. "This must have something to do with Delia's death. The blackmailer? But...why would the blackmailer want her dead? He had only been interested in revealing her secret about Shadewell."

"She might have known something more about him," Hugh guessed. "Perhaps Delia confessed a secret to her, and the blackmailer found out."

"But what secret? His identity?"

He shrugged, still as flummoxed about the blackmailing case as he'd been before. "Possibly." He stepped closer to her. "Your Grace—"

"Please," she interrupted, then turned to him. "I've given you leave to address me as Audrey."

He wished to light a candle. The evening light and shrouded windows made it difficult to see more than the darkened lines of her figure.

"*Audrey*," he continued, his voice huskier than he intended. "This makes two former Shadewell residents who have been killed."

If that concerned her as much as it did him, she didn't let it show. All she did was turn to gaze upon Mary's disturbingly still form.

"I've been thinking that the blackmailer must be connected as well," she suggested. Hugh thought it likely.

"You went to see Lady Rumsford."

She stiffened but didn't look back at him. "I did."

"She turned you away."

"Yes."

"And today?" he pressed. The duchess would not have given up so easily.

"May I open a drape?" she asked instead. Hugh assented and a moment later, gilded sunset light brightened the corner of Mary's room. It brought the individual features on the young woman's body into view: slack, ashen lips, ruined neck. Grief radiated over Audrey's expression, but then shuttered as she no doubt tried to remain impartial.

Hugh crossed his arms. "Did Lady Rumsford turn you away again today?"

"No. I waylaid her on Rotten Row. It's why I wasn't able to meet Mary at four o'clock as she'd requested. She was going to come to Violet House at six..."

Her eyes were distant as she peered through the window's glass, her expression more than just pained.

"What did you learn from the viscountess?" he asked. As he'd offered to, Thornton had sent along a recommendation, and Hugh had planned to call that afternoon, but then he'd been summoned here. It would have to wait for now.

"Why have you sent for me?" Audrey countered.

Hugh frowned. He didn't think she was being evasive. No, she hadn't heard his question as she'd stared out the window. Something was on her mind, and it was distracting her.

"Two reasons. First, the maid mentioned Mary was planning to call on your home. I wanted to know why. Now I do. Second..." Hugh reached into his waistcoat pocket and extracted a small gold band centered with a marquise cut ruby. "She was wearing this."

Her attention fastened onto the ring. "You want me to read it."

"I'd rather not involve you, but I fear you might already be involved. Besides, your talent has proved useful in the past."

With her stiffening posture and his own words leaving a greasy slick in their wake, he clamped his hand around the ring. "Forgive me. I shouldn't have asked. You'll see the poor girl's murder, and you've already seen too much of that kind of violence."

What in hell had he been thinking?

That he'd wanted her close. That he'd started to appreciate her help. That's what.

Audrey shook off the stringent set of her shoulders and chin and stepped forward, removing her glove, and extending her hand. "I don't want to see it, but if it will give us anything to go on, I'll do it. Not for you, mind you," she added hastily, as though she'd known that his reasons for calling her here had been purely selfish. "For Mary."

"If you are sure?"

She made an impatient huff and crooked her fingers. Hugh set the ring in her bare palm.

To say that her ability impressed him was too mild a way to put it. At first, he'd been utterly skeptical—no one could possibly have the capacity to see an object's memories, the events of the past playing out before their eyes. Not only that, but for an object to store memories was utterly implausible. Fantastical. And yet, Audrey could do the unthinkable. It led him to wonder how many more people could do the same, or if they could possess other mind-boggling talents.

The duchess closed her hand around the ring, her thick golden lashes lowering. Behind her lids, her eyes moved erratically. Her chin jerked back, tucking in as though flinching. The muscles forming the apples of her cheeks twitched. He longed to see what she was seeing. How much more efficient his job would be if he could. Then again, the objects she touched did not always give up information easily, or the information she wanted.

Several more moments passed, and then Audrey's lashes parted, the furrow between her eyes growing deeper. She stared at the ring. "I..."

He waited, but she didn't continue. "What is it? What did you see?"

As though it were a spider, she passed the ring back to Hugh with a shudder.

"The killer was waiting for her the moment she stepped outside." Audrey's stunned daze cleared, and she met his eyes. "It was a woman."

His pulse skipped. "Did you recognize her?"

Audrey shook her head and pressed a hand to her forehead. "I couldn't see her face, it happened too quickly. She was waiting for Mary right when she stepped outside and then...and then Mary was falling. The killer wore a bonnet, the brim deep, and there wasn't much light."

She closed her eyes, and he suddenly despised himself. She'd just witnesses a murder. Worse, she'd seen it from the victim's perspective. A victim she had known.

He set the ring on the bedside table. "Are you well?"

She peered at him, frowning. "How do you mean?"

"What you just saw—"

"I am fine," she said quickly cutting him off. She clearly didn't like being coddled. "We need to speak to Lady Rumsford again. What if she is in danger? Or her husband?"

"So I take it that she confessed to being blackmailed." Audrey had never quite answered his question. "And once again, Delia was threatening to expose the secrets of a loved one."

Audrey peered at him. "Do you know Lord Rumsford's secret?"

"He prefers men, romantically."

Understanding slackened her jaw, and she nodded. With a guarded glance over her shoulder at Mary, Audrey asked, "Will there be an inquest?"

"Yes. I'll inform the magistrate and investigate. But this isn't an isolated event. You're right, a visit to Lady Rumsford is necessary. However, I will go alone."

Her eyes flared. "You asked me here. You trusted me with this."

"Unofficially," he reminded her, though he immediately regretted it.

"Oh, I see." Her voice might have been soft, but it burned with temper. "So long as you get the information you want, my help is warranted."

Hugh stood back at her unexpected bad humor.

"You're angry with me," he observed. "Why?"

"I am not angry. I'm hurt. It's not me you trust or value. It's my ability."

Guilt whipped him, hot and sudden. He recoiled from it.

"They are one and the same, are they not? Your ability does not have its own autonomy," he argued.

She stormed past him, toward the door. Then stopped and spun back. "If all I saw when I held that ring was your arrogant face staring back at me, would you still want me here? Would you still have sent Sir to track me down and bring me to you?"

Hugh's tongue went heavy and useless. His instant retort was something he could not say. That he wanted her everywhere, in each room he stepped into. And that another reason he'd had Sir track her down and bring her here because he'd needed to be sure she was safe. But speech eluded him, and Audrey took his silence as answer.

She jutted her chin, her eyes glassy, and opened her mouth to speak. But nothing emerged. Audrey rushed from the room, and Hugh swore under his breath. What a bloody disaster.

"Audrey, wait." He chased after her, but she would not be persuaded to slow. "Please, just stop."

She hesitated on the landing. The footman averted his eyes and maintained a stoic staring contest with a portrait on the wall.

"There is nothing you can say," she replied, her voice quavering as she kept her own cool stare on the foyer below.

Damn it all to hell. Hugh tore the calling card he'd been deliberating over from his waistcoat pocket and extended it to her.

"Here."

Her eyes flicked to it. "What is it?"

"Just take it," Hugh said, his own temper now unchecked.

With a scowl, Audrey sighed and with her gloves on again, plucked it from his fingers.

"It's the duke's calling card," he said.

She sent him a withering stare, as if to say, *I know that, you fool.*

He didn't know why he was letting her have it, or what good it would do. Nor did he know how it could help dispel her fury. Maybe it couldn't. But it was all he could think to do in the moment.

"I found it in the silver case with the others," he added.

A clever light flashed in her eyes. She gave a small gasp, and then continued down the stairs and out the front door like a storm wind.

CHAPTER
EIGHT

Audrey slammed the study door behind her, startling Philip straight out of the chair behind his desk.

"Audrey, what in the—"

She held the calling card aloft, crossed the Aubusson rug, and slapped it onto the blotter in front of him. "Delia was blackmailing you."

Stone-faced, Philip nudged the corner of the card. "I did not know her name, but after our outing with Marsden to the dead house, I figured... I speculated that it was her."

Audrey's stomach plummeted toward her knees. "How could you not tell me you were being blackmailed?"

A silly question, in view of everything she already knew from Mrs. Simpson and Lady Rumsford. He'd certainly been required not to breathe a word about it.

How long would it have taken her to figure out her own husband was one of her friend's victims? No, not *friend*. Delia couldn't be that, not if she would stoop to such manipulation. She had not run into Audrey by chance on Bond Street any more than she had run into Mary. It had been calculated. A money-making venture. Though, one she had not been operating alone.

"The letters promised that should I tell you, evidence of your time at Shadewell would land in the scandal sheets." Philip batted the calling card away with a swipe of his finger then collapsed into the desk chair and rubbed his temple. "I cannot believe this. My god, Audrey, if anyone was to learn Delia was blackmailing me, and she ended up dead in the Thames—"

"You are not the only one she was blackmailing," Audrey interjected. Hugh would not consider Philip a potential suspect either, especially now that she had seen the killer was, in fact, a woman.

The vision had been quick and stilted, the attack so swift Audrey had felt its brutal contempt. The woman's choice of bonnet had hidden her face well, too.

"It began in September?" Audrey asked, calculating when she had crossed paths with Delia. He nodded. "How much did she ask for?"

He groaned and waved a hand through the air. "Ten pounds, then fifteen. I didn't know if the author of the letters— who surely was not the woman I met, given her speech—was simply starting low and planning to increase demand, or if they did not quite realize how much a duke has in his coffers. I suspect the latter."

Audrey swayed a little on her feet. All those afternoons sitting with Delia for tea, sneaking her into Violet House so as not to worry Philip, giving her expensive cast-offs... It was a huge betrayal. It certainly wasn't as though Audrey had looked forward to their meetings, but she had seen them through, and now, to think Delia had been double-crossing her. It stung. It made her feel inexplicably *stupid*.

"I presume she did not wear my cast-offs when she called upon you," she said as she stalked toward the sideboard. Oh no, Delia would have been too calculating for such a misstep.

"No, just common, workaday dresses," he replied. "She presented Lady Rumsford's cards."

Audrey poured herself a brandy and considered what Delia could have done with Philip's card. She couldn't present it to a footman, as she was clearly no duke. Did that mean a man was involved in this scheme somehow? Someone who *could* put the card to use?

"Did you keep the letters?"

"No, of course not. They spoke of your time at an asylum. Should they have fallen into the wrong hands..." He didn't finish. She understood his reasoning, though she did wish she could have held the paper and tried to glean something from it. Paper wasn't usually an easy object to read; for whatever reason, it didn't always hold energy or impart clear visions like other objects made of metal or wood or glass.

She tossed back the brandy. It cut a burning line down her throat, and she only wished it would also sear away the entire afternoon. Her disastrous forced meeting with Lady Rumsford, gone. Images of Mary Simpson's slit throat, gone. Gone would be the memories of the ring, and her argument with Hugh as well.

The insult of being summoned because he'd wanted her ability, not her, had been a staggering offense, much worse than Delia's betrayal. Lady Rumsford's comments about the Bow Street officer tricking her into believing he found her useful had inconveniently surged forward, its maw wide, ready to devour. Instead of being useful, Audrey had just been *used*.

"After what happened last April, I could not risk that the blackmailer was bluffing," Philip said, cutting into her diverted thoughts.

With the spirits now warming her chest, she set the glass down. Though at the moment his name felt like ash on her tongue, she said, "We must tell Mr. Marsden."

Philip tensed his brow and peered at her as though she had just quizzed him with arithmetic. "Are you mad? What do you think will happen if I admit that the dead woman is the very same who'd pinched me for nearly one hundred pounds? Who do you think he will look to as a suspect?"

His coloring drained then reddened in splotches. He'd been through hell in the spring. Audrey could understand why he'd panic. It did look bad for him. He had every reason to want Delia out of the picture. As did Mrs. Simpson and Lady Rumsford. The viscountess seemed spiteful and clever enough to concoct an idea to dispose of Delia, but Mrs. Simpson was far too fussy. Besides, neither Mrs. Simpson nor Lady Rumsford had any motive at all for killing Mary.

As briefly and unemotionally as possible, she informed Philip about the afternoon's events, including the murder. He had risen from his desk and paced at the window, but soon swept across the room, to where she stood at the sideboard, with alarm. She poured him a brandy.

"I do not like this, Audrey. Not one bit."

Hugh had not liked the connection either. And the suspicion that Lord Rumsford was somehow tied to Shadewell loomed over her. Had he been a patient? There had been men and women alike there, though they were separated at most times. No one would have addressed him as Lord Rumsford, to be sure, just as Audrey had not wanted her surname or relation to the Baron Edgerton known. She had been Audrey Smith there. Mary Simpson had been known as Miss Mary Wood. Delia, however, had maintained her true name, perhaps because she had no reputation back home to preserve. She had been a charity admission, she'd confessed, her placement paid for by her parish church.

"Mary likely knew something about the blackmailer,"

Audrey said to Philip. "That could be why she was silenced. I know nothing about the killer—"

"And it is going to stay that way."

She was accustomed to Philip's commanding statements. Whenever he bellowed them, she simply drew a deep breath and continued doing whatever she was doing.

"However," she said, as if he had not spoken, "I am worried for Lord Rumsford."

"And I am worried for you," Philip said.

"There is no need. I know nothing of import. Clearly—I did not even know you were being extorted for money."

Then again, Mary had been as equally stunned by her mother's admission.

She let go of a breath and shook her head. There was no use being angry with Philip for keeping silent about it all. He'd been following directions and doing so to protect her.

An errant thought struck her. "Is this why you've been so keen on adopting Cassie's child?"

He poured himself another brandy and sent her a grin that was half-puzzled, half-amused. "What do you mean by that question?"

She shrugged a shoulder. "You've been worried about any scandal at all lately. If you were concerned this blackmailer might follow through with his threat, my disappearing for a few months and returning with an infant would surely replace one scandal with another."

"Your mind in entirely too convoluted, my darling. I blame Bow Street and Officer Marsden." Just the mention of Hugh's name sent a storm twisting and turning through her.

"No. Nothing like that," Philip went on. "It's... I don't know, maybe it's Genie, about to have her child at any moment. And Michael, he seems so luminous—"

Audrey nearly spluttered on her second brandy.

"Luminous!"

"Yes, luminous," he replied firmly.

It was true, she had to admit. Her brother-in-law, Lord Herrick, was already bursting with pride for his soon-to-be-born child. She could not even imagine how enamored he would be when the babe finally came along, which should be any day now. They were waiting on tenterhooks for a messenger to arrive with the news.

Philip's tone hushed. "Have you never questioned if perhaps we were too hasty in deciding there would be no children?"

What felt like the prick of a knife's point dug into the underside of her chin. Her eyes sharpened on the duke. Her pulse stammered. Philip, however, was utterly oblivious to these physical reactions wreaking havoc through her and only smiled warmly. "You would make a magnificent mother."

Swallowing her shock, she returned the compliment, however inelegant and spluttering. Still, it was true. Philip *would* be a wonderful father.

He set down his glass on the sideboard and took Audrey's hand in his. "Perhaps Cassie's child will not do, but my idea for an adoption might just work."

Audrey jerked her hand from his. His bashful grin broke apart, and she cringed at her imprudent reaction.

"I'm sorry, you surprised me," she said breathlessly. Though she had not moved, she felt like she had just quit running at full speed. "Adopt? The title can't be passed to an adopted child—"

"It can if no one knows he was adopted. Say you make a happy announcement and then a few months later, before you begin to increase, you're feeling unwell..."

She pursed her lips. "So I remove myself to the country?"

"Gracious, no. It would have to be much farther than that. France, perhaps. Or somewhere vague in the Alps."

"Philip..." She shook her head, at a loss for words.

"Why not? We could find a perfectly suitable baby, and this option would not demand that you must carry it yourself. We wouldn't need to change the terms of our marriage arrangement. Audrey, I just want you to consider it."

His enthusiasm perplexed her nearly as much as the topic itself. He wanted to be a father? And her, a mother. She hadn't allowed herself to even believe it possible, considering their agreement not to conduct themselves as traditional husbands and wives do. A baby had been simply out of the question.

However, seeing Genie and Michael so exuberant in the anticipation of their child had affected her. Once or twice, she had, admittedly, envisioned a young boy or girl running around Violet House as Audrey playfully chased them, laughter filling the landings and rooms.

"I...I will have to think about it."

Philip raised her hand to his lips, and he kissed her knuckles. "That is all I can ask of you, my darling."

AUDREY WAS SEATED behind her desk in her study, mulling over Philip's proposal, when a knock landed upon the half-closed door.

"Officer Marsden to see you, Your Grace," her butler announced.

She leaped from her chair as Hugh entered and doffed his hat. It had been a few hours since they'd parted ways at the Simpson household, and Audrey had not yet let go of her annoyance and disappointment with the Bow Street officer. But the lurch of her stomach was not totally out of irritation, and for that she was especially troubled. She wished she could just despise him. To never again clap eyes on him. And yet at the same time, those few hours had seemed unbearably lengthy.

He stopped short just after clearing the threshold. His attention fastened to the gown she wore—deep sapphire silk, embroidered with chenille thread of a lighter blue. She and Philip were attending a performance at the opera in an hour, even though it was the last thing she felt like doing. Still, she had capitulated, if only to soften the blow of her poor reaction to his suggestion to adopt an heir. She had promised to think about it, and she would...but a child was so serious and permanent. Too many questions cluttered her mind about her ability to be a good mother, despite his assertions that she would. Perhaps if she spent more time with Philip, he would at least accept that she was not rejecting *him* in the end, if and when she said no.

Hugh cleared his throat. "You look..." He blinked. "Are you going out?"

The cut-off compliment should have pleased her, but her irritation with him wouldn't allow it—and that only irritated her further.

"Not for a while yet." She folded her hands before her. "Why have you come?"

She was being terse, and he certainly heard the ice on her tone, but he pushed onward. "Lord Rumsford was a patient at Shadewell."

She unclasped her hands. "You spoke with him?" Audrey couldn't imagine the viscountess would allow Hugh entry into her home.

He shrugged and with a mischievous arch of his brow said, "It took some convincing. Thornton sent a word of recommendation, and when that was not enough to encourage her ladyship, my promise that the horse patrol in front of her home would be happy to stay put for as long as it took for her to answer my questions sped things along nicely."

Audrey wished she'd had some similar leverage during her

interview—if one could even call it an interview—in Hyde Park.

Still peeved, she stiffened again and put on her ducal tone. "I take it you have some object for me to hold."

Insult clamped down on his expression, and his eyes narrowed. "No. I do not. And let's resolve this, shall we?" Hugh tossed his hat onto the study's sofa. Audrey watched him carefully, alarm rising when he crossed the rug toward her desk and braced his hands against the edge. "I do value your ability. And yes, it has been rather helpful in providing information and leads, but I am not standing here because I want to use your talent. I'm standing here because you know things I do not about this case. I'm standing here because you want to help, and despite my better judgment, I want to let you. And I'm standing here because I cannot seem to stop finding myself in your presence."

The air around them went as silent and as still as a portrait; a sliver in time, frozen. Audrey stared at him, heating infusing her from the center of her chest to the tips of her ears. Lips parting wordlessly, eyes blinking, she must have looked simpleminded. She had not expected a speech of such raw intensity— or the accompaniment of his steady, admiring gaze.

"I..." she began. His attention slipped to her mouth, then slowly rose to her eyes again.

Audrey cleared her throat and severed their protracted stare. "I suspect Delia ran into Lord Rumsford at some point this fall."

She straightened some papers on her desk, not watching to see if Hugh showed any disappointment in her awkward and obvious change of topic.

"At a bookshop on the Strand," he confirmed after a long moment. "Apparently, while at Shadewell, Rumsford began to teach Delia how to read and write. They spent many hours in the library there, with Rumsford often reading to her."

She had avoided looking at Hugh by turning toward the windows. Outside, evening had waned, and the windows reflected the study rather than the limbs of the broad plane tree. Just as the waft of a certain scent could conjure a specific memory, the mention of the library at Shadewell drove through her like a wick touched with a lit taper.

"You've thought of something," Hugh said. "What is it?" She realized she had been staring at the windows for too long as her memory worked.

It had been ages since she'd thought of that library, with its limited shelves and even more limited collection of books. As one of the calmest places at Shadewell, most of the residents who frequented it treated the room as a respite, a place to separate themselves from those who were truly afflicted.

"I think I know who Lord Rumsford was there," she said.

Hugh's brow crinkled. "Who he *was*?"

Audrey stepped out from behind the desk as a shivering sensation settled under her skin. A physical reaction to discussing Shadewell, surely.

"We did not all use our given names or titles, of course. Discretion was always upheld," she explained. "I was Audrey Smith, Mary Simpson was Mary Wood, and if I'm correct, Lord Rumsford was the sweet and gentle Teddy."

Looking to be somewhere in his late forties or early fifties, Teddy had been short and stocky with brown hair flecked with gray near the temples. He'd always worn a kind smile and had been notably patient when teaching Delia and a few others their letters and numbers inside the library.

"And what about Delia?" Hugh asked, removing his outer coat. The fire in the grate had warmed the room considerably since one of the footmen had stoked it earlier. "What name did she take?"

"She kept her given name," Audrey replied. Hugh nodded,

seeming to understand that Delia had not had a reputation or a life in London worth preserving.

"Why was she there?" he asked instead.

Delia's story never failed to make Audrey both squeamish and enraged.

"Her father was not kind. He...abused her from a young age. Finally, Delia's mother found them...in the act." She swallowed, averting her eyes from Hugh's. It was a horrible, wretched image to concoct in her mind, and she didn't want to look at him while thinking it.

"Bastard," he hissed, understanding again without question.

"Delia's mother accused her of seducing her own father, calling her a demon child, warped in the head and heart. He was all too willing to agree with his wife."

When Delia had related the reason for her being locked up at Shadewell, Audrey had scarcely believed it. But after a while, she had come to realize it was the truth. Delia was not like her or Mary or Teddy. She wasn't refined or reserved. Well-trained, some might say. Her language was bolder, her manner rougher.

A rare look of loathing transformed Hugh's expression into something Audrey would never wish to be directed toward her. The dark glower made her shiver, and then she cursed herself for being so thoughtless. So tactless. Hugh had been publicly accused of a crime reminiscent to that of Delia's father—the ruination of his half-sister. However, where Mr. Montgomery had been guilty as sin, Hugh had been innocent.

"Did Delia have anything to do with either of her parents after she left Shadewell?" he asked.

Audrey shook her head. "Apparently, they left London before she returned. Their departure didn't upset her."

Hugh took a few breaths and rubbed at the crease in his

brow, visibly attempting to expunge the disturbing account from his mind. Then, he got back to the case.

"Lord Rumsford claims her handwriting and spelling were equal to that of a young child's when they parted ways at Shadewell, so Delia being the author of the blackmail letters is out of the question."

Audrey crossed the room, toward the darkened windows. Her reflection surprised her; the new gown she wore for the opera looked far too elegant and chic for this discussion. For some inane reason, seeing herself in something so refined made her feel less substantial, as translucent as what she saw in the glass pane.

"Does Teddy—I'm sorry, Lord Rumsford. Does he know anything about this other blackmailer?" she asked.

While at Shadewell, Audrey had suspected that Teddy was a professor or academic, but a viscount made more sense. He was always well put together and unfailingly polite. Like many of the men Audrey had met in the peerage, he remained standing until all the ladies had seated themselves around the library table for their studies. Though Audrey did not need the lessons that he offered some of the others, she found his eloquent voice soothing to listen to from where she sat in a chair, paging through everything she could find on the library's inadequate shelves.

"No. He can't think of anyone from Shadewell who might stoop to such a ploy, and he was especially cut up about Delia's betrayal and death."

Audrey must have made an assenting expression, because Hugh crossed his arms and said, "You are as well."

"No," she blurted out before she could think twice. But then, she grimaced. "Maybe a little. We weren't close, and when we met again in September it brought back so many memories that I'd wanted to let go of. But..."

Like two strings of tangled yarn finally loosening enough to pull free from each other, Audrey realized why she'd been so unsettled since all of this began. She turned to Hugh, who waited for her to continue with a narrowed, attentive stare.

"I was there for two years," she whispered. "Sometimes it felt like I would be there for my whole life, like Lady Gladdington, this sweet older countess who truly did need to be there." Lady Gladdington had roamed the corridors and rooms, singing and laughing to herself. "But there was a short time, for about four or five months, when a few of us would meet in the library. It wasn't anything official. We'd just show up, and we'd read and discuss books, look at atlases, and listen to Teddy."

The room had been a reprieve from the rest of the austere, cold rooms. And the same faces showing up day after day had become a much-needed routine. Something she had lost since being forced away from her home at Haverfield.

Audrey reached for the nautilus shell that sat upon the windowsill in her study. The rough outer layer of the rounded shell had been thoroughly polished, to a smooth pearlescent surface, and her brother James had etched a woodland scene on both sides. Trees, vines, a hare, a bird, the rack of a buck hidden within the foliage. He'd given it to her as a gift shortly before the fever that took his life, and she still treasured it. She took it with her whenever she and Philip changed residence, treating it like a talisman of sorts. Now, she turned it over in her palm, and it calmed her.

Hugh joined her at the window. "Who else?"

She gripped the shell and peered at him. "What?"

"The others in the library at that time. Who were they?"

Of course. The library. Delia, Teddy, Mary, and herself. They were all part of the same circle at the library. It wasn't just Shadewell that connected them here and now, in London. It was the library itself.

She set the nautilus back onto the windowsill, the wide opening to its spiraled inner chambers balancing it upright. She paced away, toward the hearth, the cogs and gears in her mind working. "George usually trailed Teddy everywhere, and he would come to the library most days."

"I would have thought men and women would be kept separate," Hugh interjected.

"They were for the most part," she said. "However, we were allowed to commune in the library and during meals."

"And this George fellow," Hugh went on. "His name might not truly be George?"

Audrey sighed. "Exactly. There were a few other women—Estelle and Tabitha come to mind. However, Tabitha..." A pang of heartache struck like a viper, sneaking up on its prey. It had been years since she'd thought of the poor woman. One more memory of that dreadful place that she'd worked so hard to forget.

"There was an accident." Audrey's knees trembled along with her voice, and she moved to the sofa and sat down as nonchalantly as possible. "She somehow stole out of the building and off the grounds one night. The next morning, a search was launched, but they found her in a bog pool. In the dark, she wouldn't have seen it coming. Her legs must have become stuck and in her struggle... Or perhaps she did it on purpose. That's what everyone whispered, at least."

Hugh glowered, as though he'd like to box an opponent at Gentleman Jack's. "Did that sort of thing happen often?"

Audrey shook her head. There were precautions taken to keep the patients from harming themselves or others, and the ones who were serious about it were watched every moment of every day. She had not thought Tabitha at all inclined.

"You mentioned an Estelle. Any idea who she might be?" Hugh asked, but Audrey shook her head. She had been refined.

Definitely highborn. Audrey and some others had been suspicious that Superintendent Warwick had taken a shine to her, and she to him. But any sort of relationship with the doctor was untenable and impossible.

"After Tabitha's death, I didn't see her often. A short while later, she announced to us that she was leaving. That she had been discharged."

"So, if Delia knew Mary Wood was truly Mary Simpson, and that Teddy was Lord Rumsford...and your true identity too," he said, "it stands to reason she or the blackmailer had access to records, where the patients' true identities would be listed."

It did make sense. How else would the person have found the former residents back in their regular lives? But why now, years later?

Audrey wanted to stand but her legs still felt strange. Her heartbeat was still a little too rapid. Deep inside, she'd known allowing Delia into her life would pierce the firm boundary between her world now, and her time at Shadewell. A time she'd made every effort to forget.

"Did you speak to the duke?" Hugh asked, his voice soft.

"I did." The instant cinching of her stomach made her trembling worse. She was glad she had not attempted to stand. "He paid out nearly one hundred pounds over the last two months."

Hugh rubbed the back of his neck and nodded. "I figured that was the case when I comprehended the calling cards trick. I'm guessing your footman was presented with Lady Rumsford's card."

The puzzle pieces formed a messy pile in her mind, and she shook her head. "What an elaborate charade."

Hugh lowered himself into a chair, adjacent from her, and leaned forward, elbows on his thighs. "And to what purpose? One hundred pounds from the duke? Surely less than that from Mrs. Simpson and the viscountess."

The amount had struck Audrey as strange too. "Perhaps it was just enough to convince them to keep paying. Or..." She leaned forward, the stiff stays under her bodice squeezing such movement. "Or the blackmailer became wise to how little they were asking for and became greedier?"

Hugh considered the theory with a slow nod and distant eyes. "Possibly." He sank back into the chair, as if settling in for a long sit. He looked spent, and no wonder. It had been an eventful day.

"Sir Gabriel has dismissed Miss Montgomery's death as misadventure, but he won't be able to do the same with Miss Simpson's. Once I present my theory to him—"

"Your theory?" She sat stiffly again. "I see."

He held up his hands. "What would you have me do? There are rules. I'd be laughed out of Bow Street if I admitted to working with you. Already, they call you *my* duchess."

She sealed her lips, swallowing her ready retort. "They do?"

He shifted, no longer appearing as comfortable in the chair. "Yes."

Audrey wasn't quite sure how to feel, knowing the men at Bow Street were linking her to Hugh. Yes, she'd interfered in the case against Philip, and then the reports of the murders in Hertfordshire had found their way to London easily enough. Her summoning Hugh to the countryside to investigate had probably been gossip worthy. But were they *laughing* at her? She bristled. "I don't belong to you."

He tightened his jaw. "No. You do not."

As it had before, the room seemed to suspend in time; the air grew thick, and a muscle along his jaw jumped.

Audrey pushed to her feet, forcing her knees to lock. "Very well. If you must claim credit for all the advances in this investigation, then I will leave you to it. I wish you luck tracking down the rest of the answers."

She was being petty. He was right: Duchesses did not join in on Bow Street investigations. But this was the only way to maintain her own dignity. And perhaps, as much as she hated to do it, their connection needed severing.

Hugh slowly stood from the chair. Holding her stare, he reached for his coat and hat. What he thought or felt from her dismissal was buried, hidden behind a hard glaze forming in his eyes. His jaw still tensing, he looked like he wanted to say something. Argue with her or tell her she was being petulant.

Instead, he gave a short bow. "Good evening, Your Grace."

He was gone on her next breath. Audrey stared at the open study door, half-expecting him to come streaking back through, to say something more. But he didn't. Instead, Greer entered a few minutes later to find Audrey again holding James's nautilus in her hand.

"Your Grace? The duke informs me he is ready to leave for the opera."

The opera? *Oh.* She ran a hand over the waist of her gown. She'd nearly forgotten her plans for the evening. Audrey turned to her lady's maid.

"Pack our things for a few days of post road travel, and inform Carrigan to prepare the coach. We shall leave first thing in the morning."

Greer betrayed her surprise with a slight lift of her brow. "Where should I say we are going, Your Grace?"

"Northumberland." Her maid merely nodded as though a last-minute, two-day trip north was routine.

If the blackmailer had access to Shadewell records, then Audrey was going to find out how. To hell with her own fears of the place. And to hell with Bow Street.

She'd show Hugh Marsden, and the rest of them, what a duchess could do.

CHAPTER

NINE

"What does the bloody duchess have to do with this?" Sir Gabriel slammed his tankard onto the scarred table inside the Brown Bear, the contents sloshing over the lip. Hugh moved his hand just in time to avoid the splattering of ale.

He grimaced. "Nothing."

He didn't enjoy lying to his superior, but he also couldn't very well divulge that the Duke of Fournier was being blackmailed by the same person blackmailing Mrs. Simpson and Lady Rumsford—both of whom were connected to an asylum up north, as was the dead prostitute. After hearing Hugh out, the chief magistrate had reluctantly agreed she *might* have been killed and discarded into the Thames rather than just drunkenly falling into the river. The murder of Miss Mary Simpson, and the connecting threads of blackmail, had convinced him to allow Hugh to investigate further.

"Stevens told me the cyprian had the duchess's calling cards on her," the magistrate said. *Damn it.* Hugh had hoped Stevens would file a report and leave it at that.

"The duchess donates much of her old clothing to charity,"

Hugh replied, keeping his expression blasé. "She believes her maid must have overlooked the card case before sending off her things."

The dining room of the Brown Bear was a den of raucous activity. All around them, patrons—many of them constables and foot patrolmen—supped and drank and laughed boisterously. The place did a good amount of business, thanks to the magistrate's court and offices across the street. The previous April, Fournier had been kept in one of the rooms upstairs while awaiting a Grand Jury trial—with his vast resources, the magistrate had not wanted to release him. The duke would have disappeared into the Continent in a blink. The makeshift holding cells at the Brown Bear were still a world better than anything he'd have found at Newgate, but to the duke, it must have been the equal of squalor.

"How did you track down the dead cyprian's boarding house in the first place?" the magistrate asked. Hugh filled his lungs, mind tumbling in search of a believable answer.

The truth would not suffice here either: That the Duchess of Fournier had led him to Delia's address.

"Mrs. Roy, the boarding house landlady, reported her tenant as missing. I made the connection." It was a risk. If Sir Gabriel went looking for the missing person report, he would not find it.

"Coincidence, that," the magistrate grumbled, clearly unconvinced. "Fine. You may investigate, but Marsden, I warn you—keep the duchess out of this business. That hassle in the spring brought too much scrutiny upon Bow Street."

"Yes, sir. She will not be involved, I assure you."

At least not from this point on. Audrey had all but given him the toss the night before. Her pride and feelings were injured over the fact that he could not openly work a Bow Street investigation with a duchess as his partner, but what could he do about that? Nothing. She was being unreasonable. If he did not already know her, he would have marked it down to her being a spoiled peer. But that wasn't it. The real cause of her hurt was something buried deeper within her. He was certain it had to do with her mother and uncle's betrayal and neglect. And Shadewell.

The place loomed like a malignant black mass in Hugh's imagination. It was a place for those who did not conform to society's rigid rules to be shut away and hidden, it seemed. Audrey for her spectacular gift; Lord Rumsford for his nonconformist feelings of love. But Delia Montgomery had been sent there for no wrongdoing on her part. She had been a victim of abuse and of despicable lies. How many more residents were there for the same false reasons?

Sir Gabriel finished his ale like a man stumbling out of a desert; the whole tankard went down in one prolonged guzzle.

"The wife is waiting. She'll have my hide if I'm late again," he said as he stood, then belched loudly. He might have been a knight and a gentleman, but he was blue-blooded through and through.

Hugh saluted him with his own half-drained tankard of ale. Sir Gabriel stood next to their shared table, a quizzical squint of his eye. "You know, my Rebecca isn't much of a gossip herself, but she hears plenty of it, and she brought back an interesting story the other day. About a certain duchess and viscountess exchanging tense words on Rotten Row."

Lead ballast poured into Hugh's stomach. He sipped his ale, pretending at disinterest. "Is that right?"

"Don't think for one minute you can pull the fleece over my eyes, Marsden." He lowered his voice, but even through the ruckus of the tavern, Hugh could hear him perfectly. "My officers must be above reproach, and you are one of my best. Don't let this fancy for the duchess go any further." He tapped the table for emphasis and then strode away, through the crowd, to the door.

The magistrate's subtle warning slid under his skin as he sipped his ale. The brew soured his stomach and so he set the tankard down and stood to take his leave as well.

Above reproach echoed in his head as he walked the few blocks back to his home on Bedford Street. This was two nights in a row now that he'd returned in a high dudgeon. He'd felt like a lump of shite the night before, after leaving Violet House. But it was for the best to be done with the duchess. A partnership between them was utterly impossible. Impractical. And the more time he spent with Audrey, the more his mind seemed to conjure her as he went about his day. And hell, it was worse at night when his traitorous mind would conjure her while he lay in bed.

Damn. Gloria had been spot-on. He *had* been making love to someone else.

Above reproach. He had been, for years. Being anything but honorable and honest and hardworking would have played right along with the preconceived notions about him—from his birth to his exile from the Viscount Neatham's household. He had come too far to lose his footing now.

Basil met him at the door, and for the hundredth time, Hugh wondered how his valet always seemed to perfectly time his passing through the entrance foyer with Hugh's arrival. Basil was far too high in the instep to be valet for a bachelor with a gentleman's living. He belonged in a home of more consequence with a larger staff underneath him to direct to his high expectations. But for some reason, Basil had not yet given his notice.

"Ah, there you are—" Basil said, and because Hugh could not curb his irritation over the conversation with the magistrate, he interrupted.

"Prepare my things for a few days and hire a phaeton," he said, shrugging out of his coat and hat and letting Basil whisk them away for instant brushing and spot treatment.

"Are we leaving town?" Basil asked.

"*I* am," he replied, then held up a finger to stay his valet's argument, which was already forming on his lips. "As I will not be presenting myself to any lords or ladies of quality, my attire and neck cloth will not need a perfecting hand."

Basil had insisted on joining him in August for the investigation in Hertfordshire, as Lady Prescott had hired him and the Duke and Duchess of Fournier were sure to receive him, and heaven help Basil if he was going to allow Hugh to wander into their grand homes without a properly knotted cravat and perfectly buffed hessians.

His valet frowned. "Where are you going?"

Only the most impertinent of servants would have asked such a question of his employer. Basil was shameless, but Hugh was far too used to his cheek to reprimand him any longer.

"An insane asylum," he answered, purposefully frank in hopes of shocking him. Of course, it didn't work.

"Well in that case, I'll pack last season's trousers and that shirt of cambric I've been meaning to cast off."

"I'm not being *confined*, Basil. This is for an investigation."

He sniffed, and Hugh half wondered if he was disappointed. "Very well. You have a visitor."

Hugh had started up the steps, but now pivoted back toward his valet. "What? A visitor? Why didn't you say?"

"I just did," Basil pointed out with an incredulous wrinkle of his brow. "She arrived only a minute ago. She is waiting in the kitchen."

Hugh set his hands on his hips, more flustered than before. "The kitchen? Why would you install a visitor in the kitchen?"

Basil merely gestured toward the back of the house, giving

him the *Go see for yourself* look that he had perfected over the last few years.

Hugh stomped toward Mrs. Peet's kitchen, knowing the woman would not be there at this hour. She arrived at dawn and prepared breakfast and dinner, leaving most days around midafternoon. Hugh was capable enough to warm his dinner in the oven or to be unmotivated enough to eat it cold.

A thin, ragged looking woman sat at the kitchen table. A baby, swaddled in a frayed blanket, lay squirming in her arms. She jumped to her feet, her widened eyes locking onto Hugh as he came to a stop.

"How may I help you?" he asked, confusion holding him back from being any more welcoming. He had never seen this woman before, and the expression she wore was one of fright. A layer of dirt clung to her sallow cheeks, a darker smudge of soot on her chin. But the discolored skin under her left eye would not have washed off had she tried. Someone had struck her.

"I'm Lucy Givens," she stated. "My Davy works for you. Runs errands and such."

Hugh cocked his head. "Davy? I don't employ any boy named—" Comprehension flooded him, raising the small hairs on his arms. "You mean Sir?"

The woman bit her lip and shook her head. "My boy says he comes here, does work for you. You're Mister Hugh Marsden?"

"Yes, yes," he said, stepping forward, his posture loosening now that he understood. "You are Sir's mother? I'm sorry, he never told me his real name, so I just call him Sir."

A smile wobbled to her lips, as if the idea of her boy being called such a thing amused her. But then, her grin crashed. Tears slipped from her eyes, and a cold drizzle of dread filled Hugh's chest. "What is it? What is wrong?"

"He's in hospital," she said, her throat constricting into a rasp. The baby began to fuss. "Stabbed, he was."

The floor tilted beneath him. Hugh stumbled toward her. "What? My god. What happened?"

Sir's knobby shoulders and knees, his perpetually dirt-streaked face and unwashed black hair covered by a cap, his crafty mind and sharp eye, all swarmed in his mind as he awaited the woman's answer.

"I don't know, he's..." Her face screwed up and she fought a sob. "He's not awake. The doctor says...he might not."

At that, the poor woman collapsed back down into the chair. Basil leaped toward her side to make sure she didn't slip off the edge of the seat and hit the floor. A ball of icy fury roiled in Hugh's sternum.

She sniffled into the handkerchief Basil had produced for her. "I shouldn't have come here, probably, but I didn't know who else to go to. Davy speaks so highly of you, sir, and you've been so kind..."

Overwhelm threatened to consume Hugh, and emotion began to prick at the backs of his eyes and squeeze his throat.

"Of course, you should have come," Basil said, his own voice strident.

"Basil, hail a hackney. Mrs. Givens," Hugh said, flexing his fists, his mind racing ten steps ahead of his body. "Take us to the hospital where he is, if you will."

The next several minutes passed in a blur, ushering the woman and fussy baby into a hack and giving the jarvey the destination—the London Hospital on Whitechapel Road. All the while, questions of where on his body Sir had been stabbed, how serious his injuries, and who had done it swirled like a maelstrom in his head. Whoever it was, Hugh would crush them. He'd hunt the bastard down and pummel him to within an inch of his life.

Dimly, he realized the only sounds on the short ride to Whitechapel had been the infant squirming in its mother's arms. Sir was always going on about needing more coin for his mother and several siblings and his ailing father, though often, the mother was ailing, or one of his baby sisters. Whichever one would pull on the heartstrings more. A strange and unreasonable grin twisted Hugh's lips. Then, the band around his throat squeezed tighter.

Mrs. Givens led them into the hospital, and they were quickly directed to a male ward where patients in different states of agony and consciousness lay on beds stretching in rows through the vast room. Some had bandaged heads and limbs, others were groaning and writhing, and others looked to be sleeping. Men of all ages were placed here, it seemed, but Sir's slight figure beneath a blanket stood out among the rest. He was by far the youngest patient. Hugh swiftly strode to his bedside, growing alarmed by the chalky color of his skin. He was clean, he noted, likely washed by the attending nurses. If he'd been conscious, he would have ribbed the boy about getting himself stabbed just so he could get someone else to bathe him. Though, the amusement at the potential banter quickly fled.

"Doctor," he called to the man who stood a few beds down. He signaled for Hugh to wait and after tucking in another patient, made his way over.

"Ah, Mrs. Givens, have you fetched Mr. Givens?" the man asked, looking between Hugh and Sir's mother.

"Cor, no!" she replied waving a hand. "Davy is this gentleman's errand boy."

The doctor turned his inspection to Hugh with less warmth. "How can I help you, sir?"

"What happened? How severe are his injuries? Where was he found?"

"He was brought in," the man said, looking slightly appalled by the abrasive questions. "A woman delivered him.

She gave her name as Winnie. She asked that when the boy woke, we tell him that she was sorry for what happened to him."

Winnie? Delia's roommate? *Hell.*

"We asked her to stay, but as we turned our attention to treating him, she slipped out."

"Tell me about his wounds," he demanded.

The doctor didn't look pleased to recite Sir's wounds for him, and perhaps it was odd for a young errand boy's employer to come to his bedside and ask about his misfortune—but this was Sir. He was more than just an errand boy. Hugh had thought, he'd hoped, he would be keeping the lad out of trouble by assigning him these tasks, keeping him busy and away from the East End gangs. But it seemed trouble had found him anyway.

"A single stab wound to the abdomen." The doctor pulled back the sheet that covered Sir and displayed his bandage-wrapped torso. The boy's clothing usually hung off him; too-large shirts, surely hand-me-downs, and too-short trousers. Seeing his bare chest cramped Hugh's heart unexpectedly. He was pale and freckled without a lick of meat between his skin and rib bones. Hugh's attention drifted from his skeletal collar-bone to several bruises—new purple patches mixed with older yellowing ones—on his chest and upper arms. He glanced up to find Basil eyeing them as well, lips turning downward in a grimace.

"He's got a punctured spleen, and he's developed a fever," the doctor continued. Hugh stepped forward and cupped his palm over Sir's brow. As ashen as his skin was, he felt burning hot.

He ruffled the lad's hair before stepping away. What the devil had he been doing at that boarding house still? He turned to Basil. "I know where he was. I bloody sent him there."

"This is not your fault, sir."

Hugh shook his head, too furious to speak. The ladies had all taken a shine to him, Sir had claimed, so why then would he have been stabbed? Unless he'd seen something after all. The types of men who visited such establishments weren't expected to be saints—Sir could have irritated someone. It didn't necessarily mean he'd stumbled across something having to do with Delia.

Hugh exhaled and closed his eyes. What he wouldn't give for Audrey's ability—to be able to simply peer into that moment. See who stabbed Sir. He opened his eyes. "Where are his personal effects?" he asked the doctor.

He frowned at the odd question and pointed to a small ceramic bowl on the floor under his bed. It held just a few things: a folding penknife, a few coins, a hard-boiled egg. He crouched, picked out the knife and slid it quickly into his pocket, then scooped up the coins. He handed those to Sir's mother.

"The knife is safe with me. And these are safer in your pocket than in that pan," he told her, regardless of the doctor's displeased scowl. "I'll take care of the expense of his treatment here, Mrs. Givens. And I know you have more children at home, so I'm going to leave my valet here, Basil, to sit with Sir—Davy until he wakes."

Whatever Basil's reaction might have been to that announcement, Hugh did not divert his attention from the poor woman to view it.

She brushed away a few more tears, bobbing her head. Now, in the brighter lantern light of the hospital ward, he could see the same discolored bruising along her temple, and at the collar of her dress, in addition to her newly blackened eye.

"Thank you, Mister Hugh," she said, using the name Sir had

taken to calling him. "My boy said you were a generous man. He's lucky to work for you, sir."

He felt flustered by the woman's praise, wishing only to be able to do more for her. It was clear that Mr. Givens used his fists against his wife and son, and probably his other children too. Hugh would address that problem later. Right now, he had a more immediate concern.

"I'll find out who did this," he told her. "And they will pay, dearly."

She nodded, trusting him at his word, and after she gave Sir —Davy—a kiss on his forehead, reluctantly started away.

"I won't leave his side, ma'am," Basil assured her when she appeared hesitant to go. She thanked him, and then left.

Before Basil could start in with him, Hugh explained, "Whoever stabbed Sir might realize they failed to kill him and could come back to try again. Especially if Sir picked up something important at the boarding house regarding Delia Montgomery."

His valet removed his hat and coat and draped them over an uncomfortable-looking wooden chair next to the bed. "They won't get the chance."

Biting back a grin at Basil's stern declaration, Hugh went on, "I'll see if Winnie can tell me anything more, and then I'll head north to the asylum. If Sir wakes—" He caught himself and gritted his molars. "*When* he wakes, find out what happened, what he knows, and send a messenger to me at Shadewell Sanatorium in Northumberland."

It would take a few days traveling the Great North Road to reach his destination via phaeton, but a messenger horse could make it in nearly half that. Taking a last look at Sir's sleeping face before turning to leave, Hugh hoped to find the boy awake and well on his return. He refused to consider any other outcome.

TEN

The coaching inn was nothing elegant, and a far cry from even cozy, but when Audrey felt the coach slowing, the incessant rattling of the wheels over the rutted Great North Road quietening, she heaved a sigh of relief. They had been traveling since dawn, stopping several times to change horses, pay turnpike tolls, and take lunch at another post road inn and tavern. She and Greer had quit trying to converse hours ago and were both simply gritting their teeth and waiting to leap free of the coach as soon as possible.

As Carrigan helped her and her maid down, Audrey breathed in fresh, cool air and relished the stillness of the ground. It was past dark, the windows of the inn bright with lantern light, and her stomach grumbled with hunger.

"I'll see about securing a room for us, Your Grace," Greer announced and set off for the front door while Carrigan turned the horses toward the stables.

Audrey followed her maid slowly, rolling her shoulders and working out the kinks in her tight muscles. Road travel, even within one's own private coach, was not a pleasant undertaking. Neither had been leaving Violet House, especially after confessing to Philip where she was going.

He'd been furious and had demanded she change her mind. When she didn't, they'd had a terrible row, which ended with Philip shouting that he would have no choice but to accompany her, an offer which she had staunchly rejected.

"You can better make excuses for me here, in town. If anyone asks where I've gone, you can say I'm visiting my mother in Hertfordshire."

Not to mention she didn't want his sulky, irritable presence for the next several days of rough travel—or for when she finally faced Shadewell again, her ever-present nightmare.

"You and Marsden are going together, I presume," Philip had snapped.

"No, I am taking Greer, and Carrigan will drive us. Mr. Marsden and I are no longer going to be associated," she'd replied just as tartly.

That had calmed him, if only a degree. "Why? What did the cad do?"

"Nothing at all. It's just...best all-around for us to part ways." At least that was what she'd been telling herself since dismissing him from her study.

She didn't need Hugh's permission to investigate, especially when she was already connected to the crimes.

Philip had softened a touch then. "I agree. Audrey..." He'd taken her by the shoulders. "I do want you to be happy. To feel loved in a way I can't give you. I promise I won't stand in your way. However, if we agree to bring a child into our lives, it would not be wise for either of us to involve ourselves with anyone at this point. Especially not someone as disreputable as Marsden."

The desire to argue with Philip had been strong, and right on the tip of her tongue, but she'd also wanted to part ways for the next several days on good terms, so she'd let it go. Now, however, Philip's reasoning continued to poke and prod at her. He worried wagging tongues would spread the rumor that the child Audrey arrived home with, from wherever she spent her confinement, would be Hugh's. It smacked of hypocrisy. The child wouldn't be either of theirs!

After years of claiming he was fine with not having an heir, now Philip had changed his mind. The feeling of being trapped and backed into a corner made her stomach coil. She had not felt this hemmed in since her betrothal to Bainbury, and after marrying Philip, never thought she would again.

She entered the post-inn with the sole desire to eat and sleep and forget her awkward parting with Philip. The place was busy, with all tables filled and many more travelers standing at the innkeeper's bar. As she scanned the room for Greer, many pairs of curious eyes shifted toward her. A few stuck, though most lost interest as she searched for her maid. The crisp country November air outside was preferable to the smoky and sweat-filled inn, however a scent of roasted meat underneath it all convinced her not to step back outside and wait for Greer to find her. Audrey took another few steps, turned to avoid running her shoulders into a man—and froze.

Hugh Marsden sat stiffly at a table, his fingers rapping the wood. He glared at her.

"What do you think you are doing, Your Grace?"

He ceased drumming his fingers and pointed to the empty chair across from him. Audrey did not move to sit. The tavern's smoky air grew cloying and overly warm.

"Traveling, Mr. Marsden," she replied, hoping her surprise did not show. "Just like the rest of the clientele at this establishment."

"You thought to go to Northumberland yourself," he said, still pinning her with a look of irritation. "Alone."

"I have my maid," she replied. "And Carrigan. Wait—are you following me?"

"As you can plainly see, I arrived first. Perhaps you are following me."

Drat the insufferable man! The ache in her back and the cramping of her legs had vanished at the sight of him, but now the throbbing came back to attention. As did the need for a chamber pot.

"If you'll excuse me," she said primly, and thankfully caught sight of her maid at last.

She met Greer near the till and learned they had claimed the last available room. Greer took to ordering their meals as Audrey relieved her bladder in the privacy of a cordoned off alcove in the cloak room. All the while, her blood pumped erratically. Cursed bad luck! Of all the posting inns along the Great North Road, Hugh Marsden *would* have to stop here, wouldn't he? She certainly had not thought he'd travel the near three hundred miles from London to Northumberland, which would take at least four days there and back, in order to investigate the employees and records at Shadewell. It could be the only reason he was here. That he cared enough about the investigation to go to such lengths himself, rather than sending some constable beneath him in rank, threatened to warm her heart.

Once she had gathered her wits, and her pulse had evened to a normal rate, Audrey smoothed down her rumpled traveling skirt, tucked a wayward curl of hair behind her ear, and returned to the dining room. Still just as busy as before, the noise of the place struck her with renewed strength. A mix of classes were represented, from farmers and country women to some finer ladies sitting stiffly at a corner table, and gentlemen in tailored swallowtail riding coats and polished boots standing around the hearth.

Her eyes sought out Hugh immediately, and she found

Greer and Carrigan at his table. Biting back irritation, Audrey reached the chair next to her lady's maid. Hugh and her driver cut off their conversation and stood politely as she sat. They returned to their seats, Hugh's expression one of censure.

"The Bow Street horse patrol apprehend several highwaymen every week, Your Grace. The post road is not safe for a woman traveling alone."

"I have—"

"Carrigan offers some protection, I cannot discount that, but you should have brought at least another man—"

"I am traveling to an asylum, Mr. Marsden," she bit off, interrupting him. "I trust Carrigan and Greer above all my staff to keep that confidence. I couldn't risk bringing another, in whom I did not have such faith."

The rim of her driver's tankard swallowed his bashful grin. He was a brawny fellow and had proved to be loyal and steadfast.

Hugh exhaled and sat back in his chair. "What of the duke?"

"He wasn't keen."

He glowered. "He refused to accompany you?"

"*I* refused his company, sour as it would have been," she corrected.

The barmaid arrived right then with their supper: bread and what appeared to be cottage pie. Audrey's stomach gave a ravenous grumble. Hugh's plate had already been cleared. He watched her as she picked up her fork and knife.

"If you are finished, don't let us keep you," she said, unnerved by his inflexible stare.

"We still have something to discuss," he replied.

Greer and Carrigan stood at the same time, collecting their suppers.

"I'll go up to the room, Your Grace, to prepare it. Room

three," Greer informed her, and she and Carrigan vacated the table for a few free stools at the bar.

"That was extremely rude," she said to Hugh as soon as her servants settled away from them. Audrey speared the cottage pie with her fork. The pastry crust was flaky and golden, and she couldn't resist the groan of delight when she swallowed her first bite.

"I would like you to go back to London," he said evenly, ignoring her chastisement.

She speared another forkful. "I do not take orders from you."

"It isn't an order. It is a sensible request."

She swallowed her food and sipped some of her ale. While she would have preferred tea, posting inns and taverns had limited offerings. Besides, after a day of road travel, the ale might help her sleep more easily.

"As I am already going to Shadewell," she replied, "perhaps *you* should turn around and go back to London. If I find anything of import, I'll be sure to send a note."

Hugh sat forward, elbows coming down upon the table. "Have you learned nothing over the last several months? This is not a game, Audrey. Two women have been killed, both connected to you. If you go sniffing around Shadewell, poking into the records, and the killer learns of your interest, the same woman who killed Mary could very well come after you next."

The warning succeeded in slowing her next bite of cottage pie. She swallowed hard and touched her napkin to the corner of her lips. "I understand there is risk involved—"

He slammed his palm onto the table, causing the plates and bowls to jump. The chatter around them ebbed. Audrey sat paralyzed, stunned at the outburst. A few moments later, as the tavern conversation picked up again, Hugh curled his hand into a tight fist.

"I am sorry." He unclenched his hand and raked his fingers through his dark hair. Hugh sat back again, visibly attempting to calm his temper. She noticed then the dark smudges under his eyes, the stubble on his cheeks and chin, and the hard set of his jaw. He looked utterly bedraggled. For a man such as Hugh Marsden, a day of post road travel should not have worn on him so drastically. Worry tensed his brow, but she knew it was something more than just her stubborn insistence on traveling to Northumberland.

"I am not the only one you're angry with," she said. "What is wrong?"

Hugh lifted his eyes to hers. "Before leaving London, my errand boy, Sir..." He paused, his eyes drifting toward the backs of their neighbors at another table. Audrey set down her fork. "He was attacked. Stabbed."

Breath gusted from her lungs as she thought of the scrappy boy who seemed to be tied to Hugh's shadow. "My god. Is he very badly injured?"

By Hugh's morose expression, she gathered the answer for herself. He nodded. "Basil is with him at London Hospital. Sir was watching the boarding house where Delia lived and had said the ladies there had taken a liking to him. One of them, Winnie, brought Sir in after he was stabbed. I tried to find her to ask what happened, but by then, she had disappeared from the boarding house."

Audrey's hunger dwindled, and she folded her arms on top of the table. She peered at Hugh, wanting to help him in some way.

"He was hurt because of something I asked him to do, I can feel it," he muttered, rubbing his palm against his stubbled cheek. He looked utterly lost, and her heart ached for him.

"You are not to blame."

"I told him to stop watching the boarding house, that it

wasn't necessary any longer, but he probably hoped to find something, some nugget of information to surprise me with—" He sealed his lips and turned away from her.

On impulse, she reached across the table and covered his hand with her own. At the touch of his warm skin, she went still. An image breathed into her mind, clouding her vision, and whisking her into another room with rows of beds and men lain out upon them. A hospital ward. The closest bed held a pale boy, eyes closed, a sheet pulled back to display his undernourished chest and stomach. A bandage wrapped his torso, and bruises riddled his skin.

With a gasp, she retracted her hand. The image scattered like dust, and Hugh sat before her again. He glanced between his hand and hers, which she quickly pulled back into her lap.

"I'm...I didn't think it would..." Audrey bit her lower lip. Skin-to-skin contact hardly ever churned up memories, but when it did, she suspected it was something the person was currently envisioning. Or perhaps a most calamitous thought. A memory that plagued them, pained them, and wouldn't abate.

Hugh flexed his hand. "Did you see something?"

She gave a jerky nod. "The boy. Sir. In hospital."

The wretched thing. Far too thin and bruised. And the sight of him weighed heavy on Hugh's conscience. There was a part of London she had never known, cruel and unjust. It chewed up boys like Sir and spat them out. Life was merciless for so many.

A swoop of guilt dragged her low at the pinched look upon Hugh's face. "I'm sorry, I didn't intend to look into your mind." He probably felt *violated*—that was how her mother had described it when Audrey had been foolish enough to admit to her what she could do.

Her pulse pumped heat up her neck to her face, and back down, under the collar of her traveling cloak and dress. The legs of her chair scraped across the unvarnished wood floor as she pushed back from the table. Hugh stood roughly, but she found it difficult to meet his eyes.

"I should go up," she said.

"You haven't finished eating."

"I've lost my appetite." In truth, she had. She felt flustered by the back-and-forth with Hugh and the vision of Sir, and worse, the hedonistic pang of satisfaction knowing that the Bow Street officer would be sleeping under the same roof as her that night. She shouldn't have felt anything at all.

"I'll see you to your room," he said, stepping away from the table.

The bar stools where Greer and Carrigan had been sitting were now empty. Presumably, her maid had rushed through her meal in order to get up to the room and prepare the room. A proper duchess would not have felt a twinge of guilt over such a thing. Then again, a proper duchess would not be about to spend the night at a posting inn on her way to an asylum to investigate a pair of murders.

"That isn't necessary," Audrey said.

Hugh stepped into her path and as good as turned to stone. "If you think I am going to allow a lady to walk alone to the upstairs landing of a public inn, you've badly misjudged my character."

That same hedonistic pang of satisfaction trembled, teasing her with the truth: that his chivalrous gesture pleased her. It was wholly unlike her, to long for such coddling. If Philip had attempted it, she would have scoffed.

She feigned a look of annoyance and continued toward the back of the tavern, to the steep steps leading to the inn's rooms. A few candles guttered in wall sconces, casting long shadows, and obscuring what Audrey presumed to be the less than pristine conditions of the floor and walls.

Hugh climbed the steps behind her, the silence between

them thickening as they reached the landing. Audrey took an immediate right, which brought her to an alcove and a door—however, not to room three.

"This way," Hugh said. She turned and saw him holding out an arm, gesturing toward another corridor, to the left. Audrey followed, though they had to retrace their steps and shunt down another section of rambling hallway before finally coming to the correct door.

Reluctantly, she turned to face him and bid him a good evening.

"If you should need anything during the night, I am in room five," he said.

A delicious picture surfaced in her mind: Hugh in his room, in his bed, and in a state of dishabille. Her throat constricted and with a shake of her head, she scattered the imagining. "I am sure that won't be necessary."

They stood within the alcove to room three another moment, the muted din of the tavern below sounding miles away.

"Please reconsider," he said, and for the quickest moment, she startled, thinking he was referring to her need to find him during the night. But of course, that wasn't it. "There is no need for you to continue on to Shadewell."

With a renewed thread of anger, she shook her head. "I am a part of this, Hugh, even if you wish to push me out. I owe it to Delia, to Mary—"

"To put yourself at risk?"

"To find out why they were killed," she continued. "And to stop the person who did it."

He stepped closer. "No, that is *my* job. I am trained to deal with murderers and criminals, while you—"

"Are a duchess and incapable of anything worthwhile, is that it?"

"Do not put words into my mouth," he snapped, coming closer still. Audrey stood in place, refusing to budge or cower. But he was too close. She stabbed a finger into his chest, between the open panels of his coat, to shove him away.

"*You* came to me. *You* wanted my help! Why can't you admit that?" With every statement, she poked his chest, until he caught her hand. His fingers clamped around her wrist, but he didn't fling her arm aside. He tugged, and Audrey stumbled forward. His body caught hers like a wall, pinning her arm between them. His scent, warmed amber and male musk, enveloped her.

"You drive me mad," he said.

Heated thrill prickled her skin as Hugh held her stare, his hand a manacle around her wrist. Audrey's breathing shortened at the hard press of his body. He was all muscle and warm skin. She knew she should reprimand him, shove at him, demand he release her. Instead, a shiver raced through her as he haltingly lowered his mouth to hers.

Their lips danced together, then apart, barely touching. His other hand settled onto her waist, and points of fire erupted where he touched. Every buried desire burst forth to consume her. Audrey parted her lips on a sigh, and Hugh shattered the tenuous barrier between them. His mouth came down firmly upon hers, his lips nudging her own. They sipped at her mouth with the gentle tease of his tongue. She gasped at the sensation of it. She'd never felt anything so divine, so sparkling, as if her very blood had become effervescent.

A sound behind the door shocked her out of her stupor.

"Your Grace?" came Greer's voice from behind the closed wood door. "Is that you, Your Grace?"

Hugh tore himself away and stepped back just as the door opened. Audrey spun away from her maid. Her whole face was scorching, and blood surged through her veins at lightning speed. How could she have allowed herself to forget about Greer? Hugh cleared his throat and tipped the brim of his hat.

"Now that you've found your room safely, I'll bid you good-night. Your Grace." His voice was husky and abrupt, and his eyes swiftly met hers before he disappeared into the dim hallway.

CHAPTER

ELEVEN

At the first blush of dawn, Hugh gave up on sleep. The posting inn was a flurry of activity as the sun brimmed the treetops of the small village of Southby Green, and after his morning ablutions, he entered the stable yard. Carrigan was up and preparing the duchess's coach. The driver looked like he'd bedded down in a pile of hay for the night, his clothing rumpled and hat askew. He tugged the brim and straightened a bit when he caught sight of Hugh.

"I suspect you'll arrive in Cheltham by nightfall," Hugh said. The village was one of the southernmost in Northumberland, and where Shadewell would be found.

"That is the plan," Carrigan replied.

Hugh had a plan of his own. He'd thought it over during the long hours spent lying on his back, staring at the water-stained plaster ceiling, the taste of the duchess still on his tongue.

Since departing the alcove outside room three, his body had fluctuated between cringing with remorse and tightening in lust. He'd never intended for it to happen, but when Audrey poked her finger into his chest to chastise him, the barrier he'd erected around himself whenever she was near had pierced as easily as a soap bubble. Like an unpolished green buck, his lips had crashed against hers, his tongue practically invading her mouth, seeking out the promise of pleasure cut off at the knees in August. And had they not been intruded upon by the maid, Hugh was certain he would have dragged Audrey to his room like some single-minded brute. What's worse, from her startled but yielding response, she would have gone willingly. He'd spent the night half grateful for the maid's timing, and half incensed by it.

The near kiss in Hertfordshire should have never happened. It had been a mistake, a misstep. This realized kiss had been pure idiocy. A self-inflicted wound. Hugh ground his molars, swallowed his frustration, and focused on Audrey's devoted driver. He'd barely explained his proposal to Carrigan when the duchess and her maid rounded the corner of the building and entered the stable yard, dressed and ready for travel.

Audrey slowed when she saw Hugh and her driver standing together. A fine blush stained the apples of her cheeks, but she firmed her jaw and increased her speed toward the carriage.

"As we have the same destination, and neither of us will concede to returning to London, I suggest we travel together. There is no reason we should try to outrun each other," Hugh said by way of greeting.

The duchess, while always beautiful, looked especially alluring as she quizzed him with a skeptical look. Her dark blue eyes were still sleepy, as if she had not rested well during the night either.

"In my carriage?" she asked with barely concealed alarm.

He stiffened his shoulders, guessing the direction of her concern. Surely, she had spent the last many hours poring over his graceless kiss and how she regretted being subjected to it.

"I will ride with Carrigan," he said, "and will leave my phaeton here to be retrieved on our way back through."

Contrition pulled the corners of her lips. "That's not necessary. You should ride in the carriage with Greer and me."

He could not think of anything he wanted to do less. Should he ride with her, he'd spend the next dozen hours with the primal wish for Greer to be up in the box with Carrigan so Hugh could be free to plunder the duchess's mouth again. Either that or squirming in awkward discomfort while he and the duchess fought for a topic of conversation.

"The point is to guard against highwaymen, Your Grace. I wouldn't be much use closeted up in the carriage with a pair of females."

It was a touch harsh. The spark of insult in her eyes confirmed it. Still, it was the first brick in rebuilding a sturdier wall around himself.

"And when we arrive at Shadewell?" she asked tartly.

Hugh grimaced. To this, he had not given as much thought. However, there seemed only one course of action available to them. "We work together."

The loosening sensation in his chest surprised him when Audrey's stringent expression softened. The victorious lift of one corner of her mouth directed his attention toward her lips. Heat pooled low in his stomach. He cut it off with a cold turn of his shoulder and marched off, to arrange with the posting boy for his phaeton to be stored in place for now.

They were well underway by the time the sun had fully lifted over the horizon, casting golden light over the dewy grasses of the farmlands that the Great North Road bisected. His and Carrigan's breath fogged the chilled air as they rode along, but before long they'd warmed a little. There was no trouble the first many hours, encountering only a few drovers, a horse and rider, and a wagon off the road with a split wheel. Carrigan stopped to offer assistance, though Hugh kept his hand on his flintlock and warned him to stay ready. The horse patrol constables claimed highwaymen often staged a broken conveyance on the side of the road to lure their victims into stopping and offering help. But the farmer thanked them and waved them off, saying he had it handled.

After that, Hugh allowed himself to relax, if only slightly. They stopped to eat lunch at another posting inn and switch out horses but didn't linger long. They beat a swift path northward, their legs, backs, and skulls all suffering from the grueling pace along the rutted road. The posting inn at Cheltham was their destination for the night, and Hugh and Carrigan wanted to arrive not long after dark. In the wilds of northern England, there were no Bow Street horse patrolmen on duty, and their lone carriage would be an easy target for someone will ill intent.

Hours stretched on, and when he and Carrigan fell silent, Hugh's mind turned to how Sir might be faring. The boy was far too stubborn to not heal and wake. Who had attacked him and why continued to plague Hugh. He'd kept the pocket knife out of sight the evening before, choosing not to ask the duchess to hold it. She had already accused him of exploiting her ability. He could figure this out on his own. It had to do with Delia and the murders—he just didn't know how yet. Once Sir woke, Basil would send word. Until then, he could only try to find out the blackmailer's identity.

Carrigan stopped to light the lamps at dusk, and an hour later, the posting inn appeared like an oasis. Half the size of the place they'd lodged the night before, the inn resembled a barn, but they shuffled inside for supper and rest just the same.

Hugh's entire body ached from crown to toe, his joints stiff. Audrey silently took a seat in the tavern, her face wan, her eyes avoiding his. She refused to eat more than a few bites of bread and stew, and then retired with Greer to one of the rooms. When he stood to see them upstairs, she'd snapped her head in a tight shake, insisting it wasn't necessary. Hugh could only imagine she wanted to avoid anything like what occurred the night before and bowed his head before re-taking his seat.

He and Carrigan hired the private room in the back of the inn and spent the night stretched on a pair of couches in front of a lit hearth. The driver's snores weren't the only thing to keep Hugh awake. He wondered at Audrey's quiet, tense demeanor. He had the sense that his presence was not the only reason she'd been out of sorts. Returning to this village, the prospect of stepping inside Shadewell again, must have been troubling her.

Her silence and ashen face when she came downstairs into the tavern's main room the next morning assured him of it. Greer seemed more attentive to her mistress, which put Hugh somewhat at ease as they followed the innkeeper's directions toward the asylum.

A stone wall ran alongside a rutted path through desolate moorland and the sun stayed firmly behind an impenetrable banking of steel gray clouds. Riding up in the box with Carrigan again, a cold film of morning mist settled upon their clothing and skin. The low-lying grasses and scrub brush had lost all their color, and they passed a handful of peat bogs, reminding him of the woman whom Audrey had mentioned. The one who had escaped the sanatorium at night, only to be swallowed by the wet land. When the stone edifice of a large, blocky manse appeared from behind a rolling hill, the small hairs on the back of Hugh's neck prickled. The place looked like an abandoned castle, an austere and unwelcoming fortress enclosed by a high wall that ran the perimeter. Several gables and towers speared the bleak sky. Scores of dark windows appeared lifeless, and leafless vines clung to the limestone exterior like blackened veins.

A pair of men met their carriage at a tall, wrought iron gate.

"Visiting or admitting?" one asked. Hugh tried not to glare; this man was only doing his job.

"Neither. We are here to see to the superintendent."

"Do you have an appointment then?" the guard asked.

"I sent a note ahead." Lying might have been dishonorable, but it did not distress him in the least. The normal rules of life and society did not apply here; he could feel it as keenly as the moorland mist still dampening his skin.

The guards exchanged a glance, and then opened the gate. When Carrigan drew the carriage to a stop before the cheerless front entrance, Hugh got down and opened the door for Audrey. He was met with a wide-eyed Greer. "I'm not sure what to do, Officer Marsden," she whispered.

The duchess had pressed herself into a corner. Her eyes were closed, and her chest rose and fell erratically as if gasping for air.

"She's been like this since before we came up to the gates," the maid added.

He helped Greer down and then launched himself into the carriage. Audrey's eyes didn't so much as flutter. They were squeezed tight, her complexion pale. She breathed rapidly; her gloved fingers were laced together into a tight knot in her lap.

"Audrey," he whispered, softly and gently. He sat across from her and leaned forward. He shoved back the furious desire to pummel the Baron Edgerton into oblivion for sending his niece here, and to roar at the baroness for allowing such treatment. His heart ached for Audrey and the fear paralyzing her right then.

Hugh slid his hands over hers, feeling the vibrations of her trembling. "Audrey, open your eyes. Look at me."

Her lashes parted, revealing stark terror and panic. He held her clamped hands tighter and resisted bringing them to his lips. "This is not like the last time. You're safe, Audrey. There is no chance in hell I'm leaving this place without you at my side, do you understand? We are only here for a short while."

She blinked as if registering his vow, and her head jerked in an ungainly nod.

"You can stay here in the carriage with Carrigan and Greer while I go in, if that would make you feel safer."

"No." She shook her head. "I want to stay with you."

His chest swelled with satisfaction, though he tried to ignore it. She allowed him to help her out of the carriage, and kept their arms intertwined as her gaze landed upon the imposing stone façade of the asylum. From her panic in the carriage, Hugh expected her to cling to his arm as they made their way toward the entrance, but she surprised him. Audrey let go, flexed her fingers, smoothed the front of her traveling coat, touched the brim of her bonnet, and pressed down her shoulders. She stared at the front door as if about to duel with it. Then swept forward, to climb the wide half-moon steps.

Hugh had never been more impressed by the duchess than he was at that moment.

She didn't quail when a stern-faced matron, wearing a serviceable, high-collared grey dress with a white bib front and a ring of skeleton keys at her hip, greeted them at the door. The woman gave Audrey a long, circumspect once-over, and Hugh waited for recognition or surprise to light her eyes. But they remained stony and distant. Finally, she shifted her attention to Hugh.

"May I help you?"

"We have come to speak to the superintendent," Audrey answered before Hugh could so much as part his lips. The matron slowly returned her gaze to Audrey.

"Is he expecting you?"

"We sent a note ahead." Audrey echoed his lie at the gates

with as much ease as Hugh had shown. He pinned the corner of his inner lip to keep from smirking.

"I've not heard of it," the matron insisted, not budging from the open doorway to allow them entry.

"Does the superintendent inform you of all his correspondence?" Hugh asked. He didn't give her a chance to answer. "I'm Officer Marsden, principal officer from Bow Street, London. I have questions regarding some of your former patients."

When the woman's eyes shifted toward Audrey, Hugh could see that she did recall the duchess. Audrey, however, showed no sign of recognition. A pretense, he suspected. An aloof façade she had perfected the last few years.

After another long moment of hesitation, the woman stepped aside. "Very well. This way."

He thought he heard Audrey's sharp intake of air as she stepped across the threshold. Hugh stayed at her side as the matron showed them down a few intersecting passages. The place was as gray and dreary inside as it had been outside. Two women with lank hair around their shoulders and matching gowns of unadorned pale blue wool sat in a passageway, side by side on a wooden bench. They seemed to be ignoring each other, one woman rocking forward and back and blinking erratically. The other followed their progress past them and down the corridor with a wide, round stare.

Hugh wondered how they'd come to be there and why. Audrey had been conscripted here, and Delia too...both squirreled away to hide dirty secrets. Even Lord Rumsford, who had been arrested at a molly house, but had been able to secure a quiet release on the condition that he spend six months at Shadewell for reformation, had not truly belonged in such a hopeless place.

"Do not speak to the residents," the matron commanded.

"Some can become quite agitated. As you are aware, Miss *Smith*, are you not?"

Audrey's steps faltered, and Hugh brushed his hand against her elbow. However, she recovered quickly and replied with a thick layer of ice on her tone, "Yes. I recall, Mrs. Derry, thank you."

The urge to clap back with her new name and title must have been difficult to overcome, but sealing her lips was imperative to ensure her visit went unnoticed and unremarked upon. It impressed him too; the fact that Audrey knew not to use her title to get what she wanted meant she had learned much since her first investigation into the murder of Miss Lovejoy.

They passed a few Bath chairs, some vacant, others occupied by men and women either morose, or lost in conversation with themselves. One man raised a hand, trying to catch Mrs. Derry's attention, but the matron ignored him. Irritation barbed under Hugh's skin as she finally stopped at a door, unlocked it, pushed it open, and stood aside.

"I will alert Superintendent Mathers to your presence. Wait here."

She closed the door behind her, and the telltale click of a lock slid into place. The duchess stared at the door, her arms wrapping around her own waist. Her show of bravado trembled. She let out a shaky breath. "It is a different superintendent."

Her trepid gaze jumped around the room, from corner to corner. There were dark mahogany shelves, tall windows, a few couches, and a divan. It looked like a study one would find in any grand manor.

"This is where they brought me when I arrived ."

He couldn't control himself. Hugh joined her in the center of the worn rug, wanting only to gather her close and reassure her. And yet at the same time, he longed to punch something.

Anything. "This time is different. You're here on your own accord. Your worthless mother and uncle have nothing to do with it."

She slanted a chastising look at him. "Hugh—"

"They will receive no quarter from me for what they did."

She didn't try to persuade him otherwise. Rather, a tiny grin tweaked the corner of her mouth. It didn't last long. Audrey sighed. "I have forgiven them. It took some time, and I still struggle sometimes...but I found it helped me to let it go and move on."

"You're far more sensible than I," he grumbled.

"I might ask you to repeat that at some later point."

He didn't care if he'd opened himself up to teasing jests; at least she was no longer so starkly afraid. However, the sound of the key in the lock brought back a shine of fear in her eyes. She whipped toward the door as it opened. A man entered. He was diminutive in nature; short and slight with spectacles, thinning hair, and a pointed nose.

After a terse and skeptical greeting, in which Superintendent Mathers regarded Audrey closely—Mrs. Derry must have informed him of her previous status as patient—Hugh cleared his throat. There was no reason to step gently or to tarry, especially not in a place such as this. As succinctly as possible, he laid out the situation—the murders, the blackmailing, the connections between the victims, and finally, the supposition that the blackmailer and murderer must also be connected to Shadewell. Further, that whomever it was, had access to the records of former patients.

"I'd like to take a look through your employee and patient records from four and five years ago," Hugh went on, "during the time when Miss Montgomery, Miss Simpson, Lord Rumsford, and...Miss Haverhill were present."

Audrey took a quick glance toward him. Gratitude for not

exposing her new identity as the Duchess of Fournier brightened her eyes. Superintendent Mathers, however, looked anything but thankful.

"While I appreciate the severity of these crimes and understand the connection seems likely, I cannot provide patient files. Confidentiality is of the utmost importance, Officer Marsden," he said, adjusting his spectacles. He peered again at Audrey. "A number of our former patients would suffer undue humiliation—even ruin—should their placement here be made known."

Audrey spoke for the first time since the superintendent's arrival. "No one understands that better than I," she said, her voice steady and reserved. "Our aim is not to expose who was here, but to determine a suspect. This is a murder investigation, Mr. Mathers, and if what we think is true, there might be more former Shadewell patients currently being blackmailed... perhaps even harmed."

The man appeared only slightly moved by her speech. "What exactly do you propose? Tracking down each patient from four and five years ago and asking them if they are being extorted?"

"No, not all. Just the ones who frequented the library," she replied in all earnestness.

Bewilderment etched the superintendent's brow.

"That is the connecting factor so far," Hugh explained.

"I see," Mr. Mathers said with an unimpressed sigh. He hesitated, thinking over the request, and surely contemplating how he might be held responsible should anything go awry.

"How long have you held the post of superintendent?" Hugh asked.

"Six months," he replied, though for the heavy tone of his voice, he might have been answering six years. Hugh could only imagine the toll such a job would take upon a person. He'd only been here half an hour and already he wished to flee the bleak, oppressive air of the place.

"And has anyone come here in that time asking for patient records?" he asked.

"No," Mr. Mathers scoffed, as though the question was ludicrous.

"Then our suspect, whoever it may be, must have come before your arrival," he said, hoping to lift the burden of responsibility from the man's shoulders.

Mr. Mathers accepted this with a scrub of his hand at the back of his neck. "Very well. Wait here. I'll bring the files."

He locked the door behind him upon leaving, and Audrey glanced over her shoulder at Hugh with a mischievous, and victorious, grin.

TWELVE

S he'd forgotten how cold the rooms inside Shadewell were during the raw months of autumn. It was a pervasive, gnawing chill that seemed to grow from within her bones and spread outward. A coldness that was at first painful and prickling, but eventually dulled the senses.

Audrey and Hugh had pulled chairs to the hearth grate, as close to the flames as they could without risking one of the popping embers from landing on them. Two stacks of folios sat on the floor between their chairs—one thin stack held the records of names Audrey had recognized, and another, thicker stack were records that seemed to have no connection. They had been pulling one folio at a time from the two boxes that the superintendent had delivered about an hour ago, and she and Hugh were taking turns reading through each one together.

Hugh slouched in his chair, an ankle upon his opposite knee, with an open file in his lap. So far, their task had given them plenty to preoccupy themselves with, and they had not mentioned the kiss at the posting inn. It was for the best. Audrey had no idea what she would say about it anyhow. The truth?

That the last two sleepless nights had been plagued with unseemly thoughts of Hugh, in his room, in his bed, just down the hall from where she lay? And what it might be like to be there with him, instead of in her own bed with her snoring maid?

In the long shadows of night, she'd given free rein to her unrestrained imagination. Oddly enough, it didn't make his presence in the light of day awkward. Rather, she wondered if he'd had the same imaginings from his own bed. Right now, however, she could give no thought to anything intimate, imagined or otherwise.

Audrey basked only in the unexpected comfort of his presence. If she had been on her own, she wasn't at all certain that she'd have been able to cleave through her blinding fear in order to approach Shadewell's front door. She'd hardly been able to breathe without it feeling like she was sucking and exhaling air through a slim tube. Hugh had eased her back from a ledge, his reassurances a rope to cling to.

Now, she still felt shaky and alert, but the panic had receded.

Doctor Mathers had placed an orderly outside the door if either of them needed to leave the office but explained that he kept the door locked at all times, ever since an untoward incident with a violent patient.

"You should be quite safe in here," he assured them before seeing himself out. On the contrary, a band of panic had tightened around Audrey's chest. The mention of the violent patient had exhumed yet another memory.

When she'd first arrived, she'd been indignant, furious; her heart had felt like someone had placed it in their palm and then crushed it. She'd lashed out in anger several times, at the former superintendent, the tall and somber Dr. Warwick, the matron, Mrs. Derry, and the coarse orderlies, all of whom seemed to look at the residents as if they were plague rats rather than human beings.

How could she have forgotten the jacket? The one with the long sleeves and many straps that tied at the back, to keep her from being able to use her arms or hands. She'd fought them when they'd tried to put it on her. A hand sheathed in a white cloth had managed to clamp down over her mouth, and a sluggish haze had swept through her. Laudanum. It had made her sick for the rest of the night and all the next day. After that, she'd had the wisdom not to cause trouble, or to lash out angrily, no matter how powerful her outrage.

A kitchen orderly had brought in tea shortly after Dr. Mathers left them, and it had gone cold. She sipped anyway, grimacing at the cheap, bitter brew.

Across from her, Hugh closed the folio he'd been perusing with a slap. "George Harding, Jr., admitted a month after Lord Rumsford. You think this is the George who often accompanied the viscount to the library?"

"Doctor Warwick's notes indicate he had a speech abnormality, and the George I recall spoke with a lisp." Mr. Harding was no longer a patient, but Audrey did not believe him to be suspicious. "The killer is a woman," she reminded him. "And George isn't even in London. His home is listed as Grantham."

"This woman from your vision could be another accomplice, like Delia, and perhaps Mr. Harding has changed his residence. Perhaps he did not want to speak to those he extorted due to a telltale speech impediment."

Audrey sighed at the flimsy supposition and picked up another folio she had earmarked. Paper never retained much energy, but just to be safe, she had kept her gloves on. "Mrs. Esther Starborough, age twenty-two, admitted for extreme melancholy after the death of her infant son."

Hugh sat up in his chair and stretched his back. "Esther?"

"I think it must be Estelle. Tabitha had confided in us once that Estelle's baby had died and that she'd tried to end her own life afterward."

"Tabitha was the one who wandered out onto the moors?"

"Yes. She and Estelle were close here. But the odd thing about Esther's file is that there is no discharge date written as there are on the others, and I know she left. She bid us farewell."

Hugh reached for the file, and Audrey passed it along to him. "Could it have been left off by mistake?"

"I doubt it. These other files have been quite thorough."

He read through it again. "She is from London." He looked at Audrey over the top of the file. "Her calling card was not among the others."

"It wouldn't be," Audrey replied. "If she is the blackmailer and the woman I saw in my vision."

With a sardonic arch of his brow, Hugh shook his head. "I will investigate her when I return to London, but it still isn't clear how a former patient would have had access to these records."

The quandary was valid. Audrey didn't know either, unless she had befriended a matron here or orderly, someone who would have a better chance at access.

Hugh raked his fingers through his hair. He'd discarded his hat, even though it would have likely kept him warmer. "You could find nothing on the others you recall from the library?"

She shook her head. It seemed they had run up against a wall.

He held up Estelle and George's files. "I will visit Mr. Harding in Grantham on my way south. The town isn't far from the post road. As for Mrs. Starborough, I will call on her when I get back to London."

Audrey nodded, but kept her lips sealed. Hugh would be at least another half day returning to London. That would give her time to visit Mrs. Starborough's address herself. Approaching her might not be wise, if she was indeed involved in this black-mailing and murder scheme. But she could at the very least watch the residence from the safety of her carriage with Carrigan at the reins. Perhaps she could send Greer to the servant's entrance and ask a few questions about the lady of the house.

Still, even with that plan in place, a sense of disappoint-ment settled over her shoulders. "I suppose it's not an entirely wasted trip."

"It hasn't exactly been fruitful," Hugh grumbled, pushing up from his chair. "Are you ready to leave?"

Audrey stood, her muscles stiff from sitting in the poorly cushioned chair for so long. "You need not even ask."

"I'd like to speak to the matron on our way out."

"Mrs. Derry? Why?" She would have been happy to never set eyes on her again.

"I would like to know more about the former superinten-dent. I haven't seen his file. Have you?"

The folios scattered around their feet suddenly seemed pointless. She sighed. "No."

"Do you recall him?"

She grimaced. "Doctor Warwick. Yes. He was always so patronizing. So smug, wearing this little pleased grin...as though he was amused by all of us." She didn't understand what Estelle, who had quite openly admired him, had seen in his character. Audrey didn't like thinking of him, or the sessions she was forced to sit through while he spoke to her like she was a petulant child.

Hugh snatched his hat from the other end of the couch. "He sounds like a prat. Let's see what Mrs. Derry remembers about him."

After a pert knock upon the door, the orderly stationed

outside unlocked the office and allowed them to exit. Audrey and Hugh followed him toward the dining hall where Mrs. Derry was supervising. He led them through a few winding, narrow passageways. Patients—or residents, as Audrey preferred to call them—shuffled about. Some aimlessly, others chatting arm-in-arm, looking as though they were strolling down Bond Street for a bit of shopping. Again and again, Audrey recalled the indignity of living here. If it could even be called that.

She hadn't been living. She'd been existing. Waiting. There had been so many days when she'd feared her mother and uncle would never arrange for her release. That they would be happy to leave her there forever. She hadn't belonged at an asylum— so many of them hadn't belonged—and yet she'd been power-less to change her situation. Unless she tried to run away, as Tabitha had, only to meet with such misfortune for her efforts. She'd been laid to rest in the burial ground on the property. Even in death, she had not been able to escape. Once Audrey finally left Shadewell, she'd promised herself she would never again be put into a position of powerlessness. She'd believed being a duchess would grant her that.

And yet, she wasn't entirely free. She was still, in some ways, trapped and restricted. Oh, nothing at all like when she'd been imprisoned here in this desolate place, where people were tucked away to be forgotten. But the position of duchess had walls of its own.

The orderly led them around a corner, into a wider corridor. At the base of a wide set of stairs, an older woman sat in a rattan Bath chair. She rolled her wrists, fluttering her fingers through the air as she hummed, a smile fixed upon her face.

Audrey's feet scudded to a stop. "Lady Gladdington?"

The woman's humming fell off, and she lowered her hands to grip the arms of her chair. She sat forward, though her feet remained propped on the Bath chair's footrests. With an unexpected rush of emotion, Audrey shifted direction and went toward the older resident.

Lady Beatrice Gladdington was a widowed countess, and when Audrey had come to Shadewell, she had already been there for a decade. Like so many others, Lady Gladdington had seemed...normal. But the woman had soon proved that she was not. During the daylight hours, she hummed and sang and twirled through the rooms and halls as if at some soiree of her former years. But as the sun set, she became nervous, then hysterical, cowering in her room as she wailed about the monsters in the night coming to devour her.

Though it had only been a handful of years since Audrey had left, Lady Gladdington's face appeared sallower and more lined, as though another decade had passed. The woman's watery blue eyes peered up at her, first in confusion, then in recognition.

"Odd Audrey?"

Hugh had stopped now, as had the orderly, and turned back toward them.

"Yes, Lady Gladdington, it's me. Odd Audrey," she replied, recalling the older woman's habit of calling others by silly names. Mary had the unfortunate sobriquet "Scary Mary" for when the girl had dissolved into her fits of temper and whole-body spasms. Teddy had been "Tippled Ted" because of his rosy cheeks.

"It is good to see you," Audrey said after a moment.

The woman's bright smile waned. The brackets between her silver brows deepened. Had she detected the lie? It wasn't *good* to see her. Rather, it was quite sad. The countess would be a lifelong resident.

"Miss Smith." An involuntary spluttering of Audrey's pulse made her feel ill as she turned toward the matron, now stalking toward them. "Are you quite finished with your task?"

Mrs. Derry was clearly no more pleased to see her and Hugh than she had been the first time.

"We are," she replied, thankful they would soon be gone from this place. "However, before we go, we have a last question about the former superintendent, Doctor Warwick."

The matron stiffened, her square chin lifting. "What about him?"

"Wicked, wicked Warwick," Lady Gladdington sang.

Mrs. Derry's harsh stare cut to the countess.

"We'd like to know where he went after leaving Shadewell," Hugh said, observing Lady Gladdington with curiosity as she continued to giggle and sing, "Wicked, wicked Warwick."

Mrs. Derry inhaled deeply, attempting to ignore the teasing song. "Doctor Warwick took a new position at Bethlem Royal Hospital about five years ago."

Audrey glanced up at Hugh, and though he kept his expression bland, she recognized the twitch at the corner of one eye as that of interest. Bethlem Hospital, better known as Bedlam, was in London.

"Warwick so wicked, wicked so Warwick," Lady Gladdington tittered.

"Beatrice, that is quite enough of that nonsense," Mrs. Derry snapped. With a plaintive look at Hugh, the matron added, "Never mind this one, sir. One learns to ignore her mutterings."

Audrey glared, ready to tell her to mind her tongue. *That one.* As if the countess were not a person but a thing. Hugh entered the space between Audrey and the matron, and with a shake of his head, held out an arm to indicate she join him.

"Thank you, Mrs. Derry, you've been most helpful," he said, his reserved tone holding a trace of disdain.

With a last look at Lady Gladdington, Audrey bid her a good day, and fell into step with Hugh. His hand brushed the small of her back briefly, as if to guide her along. Warmth and a sense of protection enveloped her. He remained close, even after lowering his hand, and soon, they left the wretched building. Outside, the air warmed a few degrees, highlighting how cold it had been inside. The dull skies sprinkled rain. Audrey rushed toward the carriage, where Greer and Carrigan had patiently waited.

"Let's be gone from this place," she said to Hugh, her voice shaking, her limbs suddenly jittery and weak.

"We can stop at the posting inn where we stayed last night for something to eat—"

"No, let's keep going," she said curtly.

She needed to be as far away from Shadewell as she could get. The last few hours she'd worked hard to maintain her composure and focus on the task at hand, but now... Now, she felt as she had the day her mother had sent a footman and maid to fetch her at long last. Like she was being tricked into believing freedom was nigh and at any moment it would be taken away from her.

Hugh's hand circled her wrist, and Audrey realized how quickly she'd been walking—at practically a run. She inhaled and focused on him.

"We'll drive as far as you like," he said.

Her heartbeat slowed, and again, the fog of fear cleared. Just as Hugh promised earlier, she was leaving this place, with him at her side. No one was going to detain her. His fingers loosened from around her wrist, though they were hesitant to release entirely. It was reminiscent of the other night at the posting inn. She rotated her wrist and caught his fingers between hers.

They stood outside the carriage, rain dampening their

shoulders. Hugh's attention dropped to their joined hands. "We need to discuss what happened," he said softly.

The kiss. Audrey had known they could not ignore it forever. "Not now. Please." She did not want to have this discussion here.

He lifted his eyes to Carrigan, who was waiting a few strides away at the open carriage door. "No. Of course not." He stepped toward the driver and raised his voice. "You'll let us know when you'd like to stop, Your Grace?"

Audrey gave him a confident nod, and he handed her up into the carriage. Before he released her, Hugh flexed his hand around hers, and she met his gaze. She'd looked into his dark brown eyes many times but had never seen what she did now: compassion, brimming with stymied anger. He was furious for what she had been made to go through at Shadewell, and the appropriate person to blame was not here on which to vent his frustration. She had never loved her uncle and no longer held much love for her mother, but she did not envy them the next time they encountered Hugh Marsden.

THIRTEEN

Anticipation and dread tumbled Hugh's gut as he entered the front doors to London Hospital. The last time he'd crossed the threshold, worry over the extent of Sir's injuries had filled his stomach like hot grease. Now, he felt the same ill sensation, wondering how the lad had fared over the last handful of days. No messenger had found him along the post road as he and Carrigan had maintained a grueling pace south. Sir either hadn't woken up yet, or he had and he'd already been released, or Basil was waiting until Hugh's return to give him unhappy news.

Several pounds of weight dissipated from his shoulders when he entered the ward and saw his valet seated next to Sir's bed. The boy's eyes were closed, his hands folded over his stomach, a blanket tucked up around his chest. He appeared to be sleeping. Basil sat primly, reading with his spectacles in place. He spotted Hugh, closed his book, and stood to meet him.

"He woke yesterday, briefly," Basil said before Hugh could speak. "His fever kept him mostly delirious, but the doctor says the fever has now gone."

"Why is he still unconscious?" Hugh asked.

"They fear the fever might have..." Basil exhaled and turned toward Sir. "Damaged his brain."

Hugh gritted his teeth and tempered his frustration. The boy had already faced more challenges and unfairness in his short life than many grown men; he didn't deserve this. Other than tracking down Winnie and questioning her, there was nothing Hugh could do to find Sir's attacker than wait. When the boy woke, he could give an account. *If* he woke.

"He murmured a few things," Basil said after a moment. "I don't know if they're important."

"I'll take anything at this point," he replied.

"*Lady*, *pie*, and *Mister Hugh*."

The trio of words couldn't have been less illuminating. The fact that he'd called for Hugh, though, gave him a sharp pinch, right in the chest. He wished he'd been there when Sir woke, however briefly. Then again, he was grateful he'd gone north. They had not unearthed any startling information at Shadewell, but he'd at least managed to dismiss George Harding as a possible suspect or victim.

He'd stopped in Grantham after fetching his phaeton and found the Harding family farm in good health. A middle-aged woman, Mrs. Kemp, had greeted him and after a few guarded questions, allowed Hugh to meet her brother, George. Though older than Hugh, the man was childlike in his manner. His infirmities extended far beyond a lisp, as Audrey had mentioned.

"Our father put him in that place," his widowed sister had explained. "When he finally passed, I sent for George straight-away. He's good with the animals, and I needed him to help take care of things around here."

But it was evident Mrs. Kemp's true interest was in taking care of her brother. With George's limitations, he could not have been the mastermind behind the blackmailing scheme, and his sister had denied that they themselves were being blackmailed in any way.

Hugh had departed for the post road again within the hour, his mind turning toward Mrs. Estelle Starborough and the duchess's innocent expression when he had said that he would visit her in London. He knew Audrey well enough by now to know she was not going to sit complacently at Violet House, awaiting his report. After leaving the hospital, Hugh would return to Bedford Street for a change of clothes before setting out again for the Starborough residence.

"Did you uncover anything of import?" Basil asked after a drop of quiet.

"Possibly." He sighed and reluctantly added, "The duchess was there."

Basil whipped his head around. "The Duchess of Fournier?"

"The very one."

He and Audrey had avoided each other for the most part on the way back to London. She'd been quiet at the two posting inns where they'd stayed before parting ways, distracted no doubt by the visit to her old prison. Seeing her frightened had made him burn, both with fury and with the wild desire to ride to Haverfield and blacken both of Lord Edgerton's eyes. And while he could do nothing to Audrey's wretched mother, she was as much to blame and just as repulsive.

The need to protect the duchess, to avenge her, had lodged in the center of his chest. It still lingered. He shouldn't have mentioned the duchess to Basil; like Thornton, he already thought associating with Audrey was a foolish risk. If his valet had any idea how close Hugh had come to dragging her to his room at that first posting inn, he would have had a conniption.

"Mrs. Peets is keeping you fed, I see," Hugh said, spying the empty basket on the floor along with a leather traveling satchel.

"She agreed to stay on at Bedford Street in my absence. I can only imagine the dust accumulating upon everything." Basil sniffed. "The last four days have been a torture. This chair. That little cot there." He gestured to the cot set up next to Sir's bed. "The *odors*," he added, a green cast flooding his coloring.

Hugh clapped him on the shoulder. "Thank you for staying. I know it can't have been easy. I'll relieve you from watch duty soon. I just have one stop to make."

Basil grimaced, re-opened his book, and with a dramatic sigh, sat back down. Hugh left before Basil could remind him that this went far beyond the general duties of a personal valet.

Most likely, Sir was safe from any outside danger. Whoever had stabbed him probably wasn't going to come into the hospital to finish the job more than four days later, but it wasn't a risk Hugh was willing to take.

Evening had fallen and with it came a thick brume. It chilled the air, and by the time Hugh delivered the hired phaeton back to the livery stables and walked the few blocks home to Bedford Street, the tips of his fingers were numb with cold, his clothing damp from the fog.

The moment he stepped inside the warm foyer of his home, Hugh remembered what day it was. Friday. *Damn.*

He had barely removed his hat when Gloria appeared within the entrance to his study.

"You forgot," she said, leaning against the doorjamb and crossing her arms. In her hand was a short tumbler filled with the single malt whisky he kept in a crystal decanter on his desk.

"I am sorry," he said, shrugging out of his own overcoat since Basil was not at home to do it for him. His valet preferred to whisk his outer trappings away to a place where they would receive nary a wrinkle. Hugh tossed his coat over the newel post.

Gloria met him at the study entrance, her dark-eyed glare playful rather than irritated.

"You've never forgotten me before."

"Things are a bit...out of order at the moment."

"A case?" she guessed.

He poured himself a drink and tossed it back. Grimacing, he nodded. Catching a glance of the clock, he realized he was over an hour late for his usual appointment with Gloria. With a spike of guilt, he also realized he was feeling anything but amorous. The day had spent him, and it wasn't over yet. He had to pay a call on Esther Starborough, though it was past a fashionable hour for calls, and he anticipated it would go nowhere, just like his visit to George Harding.

Gloria rose from the chair and came to his desk. She rubbed his shoulder before leaning forward and taking the lobe of his ear between her teeth.

A stone settled into his throat and chest, sinking fast to his gut. *Fuck.*

"Gloria." He gently peeled her from his side. "I am sorry, but I'm only here for a change of clothing. I have an investigation—"

"I will help you change," she said, plucking the drink from his hand and setting it aside. "Let's go upstairs."

His mind wheeled and floundered as she took his hand and led him toward the stairwell, as she had done countless times. It was a well-worn path to his room, Gloria having been the only woman to cross the threshold in nearly two years. However, as they entered his room now, and Gloria drew closer, Hugh's mind retreated to the posting inn alcove outside room three. He could not believe what he was about to say, but it came off his tongue just the same.

"I can't tonight."

"Hugh Marsden." She fell back onto her heels and stared up at him in wonder. "Are you telling me to go home?"

Hell. Hugh clenched his jaw and scrubbed a hand over his

eyes. "You do not have to leave, but I can't stay. I'm investigating two murders that are connected and—"

"Who is it?"

He paused. "You wouldn't know them, I'm sure."

She tapped his shoulder, almost playfully. "Not the murder victims. The woman you are sleeping with."

He lost the ability to speak for a moment as he stared at her. Then, fumbling for a reply, said, "I'm not sleeping with anyone else."

Gloria chuffed a laugh and eased away from him. He frowned at the barbs of irritation under his skin.

"I am not lying. We have an agreement, Gloria, and I am a man of my word."

Kissing the duchess had hardly been a violation of their arrangement. Though, not for the first time, he regretted his moment of weakness. It was as if the darkness of that upstairs alcove had given them permission to trod over the boundaries of propriety and convention. It had erased their different positions in society and all the reasons a kiss like that would be impossible by the light of day.

"It is the duchess, isn't it?" Gloria asked as she wrapped an arm around the post of his bed. She looked utterly tantalizing and seductive, and yet, Hugh stayed where his feet had sealed to the floor.

"I don't know what you mean."

She shook her head. "Lying is beneath you."

It was. Hugh went to the decanter he kept on his bedside table and splashed some whisky into a glass. It seared his throat, and he relished it. "I am not sleeping with her."

"She could take you as her lover," Gloria said with a blasé lift of her shoulder. There was no show of jealousy or possession. Just straightforward honesty. With a surprising pinch of injury, he came to understand the stark truth of Gloria's feelings. Their long-standing arrangement might have been an intimate one, but she was not enamored with him any more than he was with her. Of course, there had never been any talk of love or admiration. Theirs was a relationship of pleasure and sometimes companionship. But her suggestion still somehow dazed him.

"Duchesses do not take Bow Street officers as their lovers," he finally managed to reply.

And with another burst of startling clarity, he knew in his soul that he would never consent to such an arrangement. He had far too much pride.

"Whatever you say," Gloria said lightly. She came to him, kissed his cheek, and then took her leave.

Hugh listened to her footfalls growing fainter, the shutting of the front door, and the silence of the house. Without needing her to say it, he knew she would never come back.

FOURTEEN

Esther Starborough's home in Kilburn, just west of Regent's Park, was not a fashionable address, but it was neat and well-kept, and solidly middle class. It reminded Audrey of Hugh's modest home on Bedford Street, in fact. As she viewed the brick and stone home from where she sat within her carriage, she again strove to push the Bow Street officer from her mind. It had been no easy task since her return to Violet House earlier that afternoon. She'd wanted to beat Hugh to Esther's home, and in rushing through a bath and allowing Greer to dress her and style her hair *without* rushing, all she had managed to do was keep the man in the forefront of her mind. As if he had not already taken up permanent residence there as of late.

It did not help that Philip hadn't been at home to distract her with any complaints or questions. She hadn't expected a warm welcome from him, but she had expected him to at least be there. Instead, his valet informed her that the duke had left the evening before and had not yet returned. With a ball of ice lodged in the pit of her stomach, Audrey had at last called for Carrigan to ready the coach.

During the long, bumpy ride back to London, Audrey had determined that sending Greer to the servant's door at the Starborough's home was too much of a risk. If, in fact, Esther did have something to do with the blackmailing and murders, Audrey would not endanger her maid. No, if she wanted information, she would get it herself—with Carrigan at her side, of course. Hugh could not launch a diatribe against her if she brought male protection. However, she was beginning to think what he truly meant by male protection was *his* protection. With great reluctance, even within her own mind, Audrey had to admit she liked the idea.

Upon leaving Shadewell, Carrigan had spurred the horses on for several more miles than was probably wise to a posting inn far enough south for the grip of the asylum to loosen around Audrey's throat. But only on the second night on the road to London did she feel as though she could truly breathe again.

She and Hugh had not discovered much and for that she had been greatly disappointed. But another part of her was relieved that she had finally, at long last, faced her fears of that wretched place. It had been messy—she had panicked. She had lost her composure. But now, the asylum and her memories of it did not loom so ominously in her mind. She had, hopefully, put that part of her life firmly behind her.

Though perhaps that would not be totally possible until after they had caught the murderer.

With afternoon sunlight quickly fading, the windows of Esther Starborough's home lit with lamplight. She'd been sitting within the carriage for nearly half an hour, and finally her impatience had burned through her cautiousness.

"Carrigan," she called, and her driver instantly climbed down from the box. He'd surely been chomping at the bit to do something other than sit there with night falling.

The door opened and he helped her down. "Your Grace, if you don't mind my cheek, I don't believe Officer Marsden would approve of this."

During their few days traveling along the post road, Audrey had suspected Hugh had informed her driver on the basics of the case. Blackmailing. Murder. Perhaps even that the murderer might be a woman. And while Greer and Carrigan knew they had visited an asylum, she did not quite know if they understood her own connection to it. Though if they suspected, she trusted they would keep her confidence.

"I don't mind your cheek," she replied. "However, I am also not curbing my actions. I value your presence, Carrigan. I count upon it."

He relented with a nod. "Very well, Your Grace."

Audrey took the lead and approached the home. The front steps were swept, and the glossy black paint upon the door held a high varnish. There would be no sending Carrigan first with her card to see if the lady was at home to receive her. It was imperative that Audrey catch Esther by surprise. Carrigan brought the brass knocker down upon the plate, and with the sensation of being tossed about in a heavy wind, not unlike when she knocked upon the door to Shadewell, she waited.

The introductory phrase she had spent hours reciting in her head, vanished into thin air as the door opened and a short woman wearing a mob cap and a dubious expression greeted them.

"Mrs. Esther Starborough," Audrey blurted out. "I am here to speak to her."

Her face heated as she heard the unpolished demand and realized she had not even introduced herself.

"My name is Miss Audrey Smith. Mrs. Starborough and I knew each other long ago," she quickly amended.

Still, the woman's expression remained furrowed with shock.

"This is the Starborough residence?" Audrey asked after another moment of silence from the woman.

"Yes," she finally answered. "But...begging your pardon, miss, did you say Mrs. *Esther* Starborough?"

Audrey nodded. "That's right."

The woman pressed her lips together with a look of concern but stepped aside. "Do come in, Miss Smith. If you will please just wait here."

Audrey and Carrigan stepped into the narrow front lobby, and the woman, likely the maid, closed the door and then bustled up the stairs, out of sight.

"Something isn't right, Your Grace," Carrigan said, his low tenor cautious.

Audrey did not sense danger, but her driver was correct. The woman had seemed alarmed at the mention of Esther.

Muted voices upstairs traveled down to them, and Audrey strained to hear what was being said. Then, the maid reappeared on the steps. Descending behind her was a man. He was pulling his coat collar as if he'd just tossed it on. He walked with the assistance of a cane to aid a pronounced limp. Despite the limp and his brown hair, centered with a graying sweep near his high forehead, he appeared to be no more than forty. A pair of spectacles sat perched upon his thin nose, and his narrow face was clean-shaven. Both he and the maid wore expressions of confusion and something else. Not alarm, but apprehension.

"Good evening, Miss Smith," he said. "I am John Starborough. My maid tells me you've come to visit...Esther?"

The pause at the end of his question raised a suspicion.

"That is correct, Mr. Starborough. I knew Esther many years ago and thought to pay her a call," she said.

"I am not sure how you were acquainted with her—"

"Is she not at home? Should I return at a better time?" she asked, hoping to deter any queries about where she and Esther had become acquainted. Any mention of Northumberland or Shadewell might cause him to turn her out.

"I am afraid, Miss Smith, that Esther is not...she is in fact no longer with us." Mr. Starborough adjusted his spectacles, looking to the floor in order to give Audrey a moment to absorb the announcement.

She held her breath and fought the uncharitable sensation of frustration over meeting yet another closed door in hunting down the blackmailer. "Do you mean to say she has died?"

"That is correct, miss. I am sorry to bear such sorry news to you." He lifted his brows, causing creases to stack along his forehead. "Forgive me, it has been some years since I've spoken of Esther or have needed to inform someone of her passing."

Audrey frowned. "How long ago was this?"

The maid lowered her head and clasped her hands before her, and Mr. Starborough again touched his spectacles. He was uncomfortable. Nervous. Audrey watched him closely.

"Nearly five years ago now," he answered.

The closed door she'd just run into seemed to creak open again. Nearly five years ago, Esther had been at Shadewell.

"How did she die?" Audrey asked. The question, bold and rude, drew looks of shock from both Mr. Starborough and his maid. "It is only that she was so young," she added.

"Yes, quite," he said, growing more agitated. He cleared his throat. Hitched his chin. Hugh had once said women hitch their chin when they are about to lie. Did that also apply to men?

"Esther passed during childbirth," he answered flatly. "It was kind of you to pay a call but as you can now see—"

"I have not been quite honest with you, Mr. Starborough," Audrey interjected. Lies would only close that door again. "And you have not been quite honest with me."

He blinked. "I beg your pardon?"

"I know that Esther was in Northumberland five years ago at a place called Shadewell," she said, finished with tiptoeing around the truth.

The maid's rounded eyes and gasp were artless and telling.

"How dare you—" he began.

"I am not here to cause havoc, Mr. Starborough, I assure you. And I have no intention of making your wife's placement there known to anyone. But I must ask—has anyone else come here recently, inquiring about Esther? Or perhaps intending to extort money from you?"

The man gawped at her. "What nonsense is this?"

The genuine reaction assured her that he had not been a target of the blackmailer. But then, why would he lie about Esther's death?

"I would like to speak to Mrs. Starborough," she said with as much ducal poise and firmness as she could manage.

The man before her stood taller, his shock simmering over to anger. "I have told you, Miss Smith—she is dead!"

Again, his reaction was utterly genuine.

"But not in childbirth," she pressed.

His nostrils thinned as he inhaled deeply and then ripped off his spectacles. "No. How do you know this? Who are you?"

"I knew Esther at Shadewell," she admitted. "And I also know she was discharged and sent home."

"You know nothing at all," he replied, his agitation heightening. "She did not come home!"

His voice broke on those last words, and a pang of shock and sadness tolled in Audrey's chest. She was now the one gawping at him. It made no sense. Esther had come to them in the library. She had said goodbye.

"I should never have sent her there," Mr. Starborough continued, his voice strained with emotion. The maid touched his arm lightly. "I thought it was the only way to help her, to stop her from harming herself after the baby died. I refused to send her to Bedlam, that awful pit. Esther's doctor suggested Shadewell. Said it was a better place. Secluded and safe..."

He squeezed his eyes shut and pinched the bridge of his nose.

"You did what you could, sir," the maid said softly.

"It didn't stop her!" he all but screamed. The maid retracted her hand, and Carrigan took a step closer, as if preparing for Mr. Starborough to lash out. But he didn't. Instead, he seemed to crumple.

Audrey drew in a deep breath and chanced another question. "How did she die?"

To her relief, he did not anger. He calmly placed his spectacles back on. "She managed to escape the building one night. In the darkness, she couldn't see where she was going."

A bubble of alarm began to rise in Audrey's esophagus. Hot with confusion, she listened to the rest of Mr. Starborough's all-too familiar sounding account.

"A search was launched for her at dawn when they found her bed empty. They think she must have fallen into one of the bogs in the surrounding moors. Her cloak and hat were found in the mire, but they said her body could not be recovered."

The front hall filled with thick silence. Audrey's throat went dry as she recalled the circumstances around Tabitha's death. They were a match to what Mr. Starborough had been told about his wife.

"Who told you this?" she asked, just as a thumping sound from the upper floor pierced the quiet. As if something heavy had been knocked over. Audrey looked up the stairs, to the landing. Mr. Starborough followed her gaze, as did the maid.

"The superintendent, of course," he answered, seeming to regain a bit of his annoyance with her. "In a letter. There was no body..." He sniffed and straightened. "Now, Miss Smith, if you will kindly take your leave. My new wife is upstairs and is not feeling well. I must go to her."

The maid's eyes widened as he limped to the door and held it open. It was incredibly rude to turn someone out so hastily, but Audrey supposed she had also been quite rude in her manner while questioning him. She moved on numb legs, Carrigan still at her side. "Of course. My condolences, Mr. Starborough."

There was nothing left to say to him, or to learn from him. As she left the residence and Carrigan helped her back into the carriage, she pored over what Esther's husband had revealed.

He believed his wife had walked out onto the moors and drowned in a bog. Just as Tabitha had a month or so before Esther had bid Audrey and the others a farewell, explaining that she was being discharged to return home. And it had been Doctor Warwick who had informed Mr. Starborough of the unfortunate circumstances.

"To Bedford Street," she told Carrigan.

The evening hour was late, and the lamps brightened the dark streets as they traveled east from Kilburn, but the urge to divulge what she'd discovered could not be overcome. Hugh would hopefully be at home by now, and once he got past his inevitable vexation at her visit to the Starborough home, he would certainly ponder with her over possible reasons behind the superintendent's deceit. As unenthusiastic as she was to submit to Hugh's displeasure, she was equally eager to share what she knew.

It was not until Carrigan had pulled alongside the curb out front of number nine and gone to summon Hugh to the carriage that Audrey considered that they might also need to trip over a discussion regarding their kiss at the posting inn. Her eagerness faded drastically and all but vanished when she saw Hugh coming toward the carriage. She slid back along the bench, further from the door as he opened it and climbed in.

The dim light from a lamppost's gas jet exposed the twist of annoyance on his face. "Are you on your way to Esther Starborough's home, or on your way from it?" he asked brusquely.

She was glad for the instant squabble, for it took away any chance they might discuss the kiss. "How did you know I would go?"

"You are not as furtive as you imagine, duchess." He sighed and held up his hands, as if waiting. "Well?"

His short, impatient manner led her to think something had happened with Sir.

"Is the boy still in hospital?" she asked.

"Don't avoid my question."

"Don't be an arse. I'm asking because I care, and you're clearly upset."

Hugh held her incensed stare as insult pricked at her. Did he really think so little of her that she would use false care for Sir as a shield?

Tension went out of his shoulders, and he sat back against the squabs. "I'm sorry. Yes, he's still there. Basil is watching over him."

She was glad to hear the boy had not taken a turn for the worse and waited until her pulse had slowed before speaking again. "Nearly five years ago, Mr. Starborough was told his wife wandered away from Shadewell and drowned in a moorland bog."

Hugh went still. Then jacked forward. "That is how the other woman, Tabitha, died, is it not?"

She nodded, the truth finally seeping in. "Doctor Warwick lied to Mr. Starborough. He used the circumstances surrounding Tabitha's death to weave a fiction about Esther's misadventure."

"Did the husband not care to collect her body?" Hugh asked, his focus razor sharp.

"There was no body, he was told. Just some evidence of her clothing stuck in the bog. Some of them are vast and deep." She had heard stories of cows and sheep getting stuck in them, the mire too thick and binding for farmers to do anything more than watch them sink out of sight, to their deaths.

Hugh scraped his palm along his jaw. "So, it would stand to reason a body might never be found. Convenient."

A sickening cramp in Audrey's stomach would no longer be ignored. "I think I know why Doctor Warwick lied. And where Esther has been these last five years."

FIFTEEN

Hugh hadn't trusted that the duchess would not set out for the asylum on her own the following morning, as soon as dawn crested the western horizon, so he had spent the night in the mews behind Violet House, bunking with Carrigan and the other stable hands. The entire way from Bedford Street to Curzon, she had accused him of being absurd, mistrustful, utterly infantile, and the entire ride, Hugh had simply sat across from her, allowing her to vent her spleen, without making a single remark.

"Why aren't you speaking?" she had finally asked.

"And ruin the entertainment? You are quite diverting when incensed," he'd replied, and it wasn't entirely untrue. He'd been forced to subdue multiple grins as she cited all the reasons why he should trust her by now.

That she had just rushed to visit Esther Starborough's home before he could return to London and do so himself, even though she had considered Esther a prime suspect, apparently did not count as untrustworthy. Audrey had not appreciated the comment when he'd voiced it and had not uttered another word for the rest of the short trip. Before she could depart from the carriage, Hugh had reached for her arm. She'd drawn back, as if burned. Discomfited by her reaction, he'd waited a few moments before speaking so he would not shout or say something stupid.

"You could have gone straight to Southwark tonight to visit Bedlam on your own. Instead, you came to me." The next words had been as difficult as shaping cold metal. "Thank you."

Her surprise had matched his own. She'd softened enough to bid him a good night, and as evidence of her forgiveness, a footman brought clean bedding and supper to him soon after. He'd slept surprisingly well in the bunk room above the mews, and he wondered more than once if it was due to the ease he felt at being so close to Violet House.

The following morning, he woke early and was not at all astonished when Carrigan informed him that the duchess had requested a carriage.

With Greer at Audrey's side, the three of them had set out for Bethlem Royal Hospital just after breakfast. One of the oldest asylums in the country, the hospital had been located in Moorfields, north of the city for well over a century. The new location in St. George's Fields was supposed to be a shining example of charity for the people of London, gifted to them by an act of Parliament, however Hugh's occasional outings across the river the last few years, to deliver both men and women to the new wing for the criminally insane, had not convinced him that the place was a gift. Unlike Shadewell, the patients here truly were treated as prisoners—as animals, even—many of them chained and manacled and unclothed.

After crossing the Thames and traveling south toward St. George's Fields, Hugh had informed Audrey that he would be going into the asylum alone.

Her pique had instantly flamed. "If you think I am going to sit in this carriage while you speak to Doctor Warwick—"

"*Audrey*." He had not meant for his tone to be so deep and final, but it had been. She and her maid had stared at him, their lips parted. Hugh leaned forward.

"This is no Shadewell. This is a public asylum. People are not mistakenly sent away here."

She was not deterred. Not that he'd really thought she would be. "I will make my own decisions, Hugh Marsden."

And so, when their small conveyance approached the long drive off Lambeth Road, toward the stark, blocky institution, he had sat back and saved his breath.

A solid brick, ten-foot wall and intermittent iron fencing surrounded the yard and the three-story neoclassical monstrosity. The wide lane fronting the hospital teemed with foot and carriage traffic, all the passersby taking not so much as a sideways glance at the place. Carrigan pulled to the curb as the only way in would be on foot through a slim gate fronting the entrance court. Assuring Greer that she would be just fine, Audrey left her with Carrigan and approached the gated lodge with Hugh. A guard posted there inquired after their business and when it was clear they were visitors, allowed them entry.

On the far side of a tree-lined court, wide steps led to a columned portico. Hugh noted Audrey's silence as they walked toward it, their shoes crunching over the small stone gravel.

"Have you been here many times?" she finally spoke, her words noticeably tremulous.

"Several," he replied. "There are wings for the criminally insane. They are kept apart from the other patients."

Her pace slowed, and Hugh was forced to stop and turn back to her. Her stare was hinged on the grand entrance, and she seemed to be taking deeper breaths than usual. It was not as panicked as she'd appeared at Shadewell, but similar.

"Audrey," he said softly, then, before he could stop himself, extended his hand.

Her eyes lowered from the building to his gloved hand. She then peered at him. "You're not going to tell me to go back to the carriage?"

"Would you if I did?"

"No."

"I did not think so. Take my hand."

Her lips pressed against the smile trying to form as she slid her gloved fingers through his. They resumed walking, Audrey quickly shifting her hold from his hand—which was certainly too intimate—to the crook of his arm. They took the steps, and an attendant met them on the portico.

"We are looking for Doctor Warwick," Hugh said, and because they needed a reason, and because Warwick might scatter off into the depths of the asylum should he hear a Bow Street officer was looking for him, he added, "My sister and I are searching for a convalescent home for our dear poor mother."

Hell, now he sounded like Sir.

The attendant nodded and showed them into the entrance lobby, which opened ahead to a main stairwell.

"Wait here," the man said, and then departed.

"It's enormous," Audrey whispered, still holding his arm. She then whispered, "*Brother*."

Mischief lit her eyes, and Hugh stifled a grin. "Yes, well, dear sister, only the best for our beloved mum."

She pinched him through his coat just before the attendant returned with another man. He was likely in his middle thirties, with blond hair, handsome looks, and a direct stare. He wore a charcoal suit and waistcoat, a neckcloth and winged collar, and had the starched expression of a man with a thankless, exhausting job. At his arm, Hugh felt the duchess tense. This was indeed Warwick.

"Good day and welcome," the doctor said. His eyes landed on Audrey, then shifted to Hugh before darting back to her again. He blinked and frowned. "I am told you are here in regard to your mother?"

He likely recognized Audrey but could not place her. To her credit, she bit her tongue. They were much too close to the front doors to risk coming clean with the truth. The attendants here were used to handling all manner of problematic men and women, and with one word from Warwick, could easily shunt them out the door.

"Yes, doctor, this is a rather difficult topic for us." Hugh lowered his voice. "If we could discuss the particulars somewhere more private?"

With the flair of a stage actress, the duchess whisked out a lace kerchief and pressed it to her nose before sniffling. Hugh fought a roll of his eyes and a bark of laughter. Doctor Warwick assured them he quite understood and led them to his office, just past the entrance lobby. When at last they were closed inside a private room, the windows of which overlooked the portico, front court, and the slate gray November sky, Hugh shed the act.

"Doctor Warwick, am I correct that you were superintendent at Shadwell Sanitorium in Northumberland several years ago?"

The doctor had come to stand behind his desk, and now, his fingers pressed into the polished wood surface.

"That is correct," he said, slowly and skeptically, likely still wondering if this was about their mother. "Are you familiar with that institution?"

"I am." Audrey released Hugh's arm and stepped forward, across the carpet. "Doctor Warwick, you may not recognize me, but I was a patient at Shadewell when you were superintendent."

He perused Audrey's face with a narrow eye, apprehension wiping away all pleasantness on his expression.

"Miss Haverhill. Yes, of course, I do recall you. What is this about?" He skewered Hugh with a glare. "You do not have a mother in need of care, do you?"

"I'm afraid not," he replied. "I'm a principal officer at Bow Street, and I'm investigating a blackmailing scheme in connection with two murders."

As if his legs suddenly became gelatinous aspic, Doctor Warwick swayed. He dug his fingers harder in the desk.

"Murders?" He licked his lips. "I do not know what this could possibly have to do with me or Shadewell."

"The victims have been former residents," Audrey said.

His aspic legs gave out. Doctor Warwick collapsed backward, into his chair. "Dear God, no. Please tell me it is not—" He swallowed the rest of his sentence, but Hugh finished it for him.

"Esther?" More color drained from the man's face. "No. Two other women have been killed."

The doctor's visible relief irritated Hugh. Though he did not wish death upon anyone, especially no woman, the doctor's dismissal of two other murdered women was in poor, selfish taste.

"I visited Esther's home in Kilburn yesterday and learned of your deception," Audrey continued. "You led her husband to believe she was dead, and I'm willing to wager it was because you and Esther plotted to abscond together. You met with her here in London when you took this position."

As he stammered over the beginning of his reply, Hugh was reluctantly impressed with how unnerved the doctor already appeared to be.

"You do not understand," Warwick finally said without spluttering. "Esther and I did not mean to fall in love. Her time at Shadewell changed her. It made her realize that she was not happy with the life she'd had before. And the more time we spent together...it was as though we had been searching for each other for our whole lives."

"She was a married woman. A patient at your hospital, under your care," Hugh said, less than sympathetic to the man's reasons. "Did you never think that your authority might have swayed her into believing she was in love with you?"

Doctor Warwick shot to his feet. "No! Esther does loves me. She is my wife—"

"As she is still legally married to Mr. Starborough, she is *not* your wife," Hugh cut in.

"Your duplicity is not our main concern at the moment, however," Audrey said. "Where is Esther? We must speak with her."

The doctor's fear whether Esther was one of the murder victims now caught up to Hugh. "You don't know where she is."

Doctor Warwick gaped at him. "How did you know that?"

Explaining how he'd deduced it wasn't worth the time it would take. "When did you last see her?"

The doctor loosened his neckcloth, his hand trembling. The man was coming apart at the seams. Before he'd even given an answer, Hugh knew Esther had been missing for some time, and that the doctor had been covering up her absence.

"A fortnight," he confirmed.

Audrey and Hugh crossed a look. Two weeks. Just about the time Delia Montgomery went into the Thames.

"Have you not reported her missing?" Audrey asked.

Doctor Warwick tossed up a hand. "How can I? They might print her name and likeness in the news sheets. Starborough could see it. The police might ask questions I cannot answer."

Hugh nodded; the doctor was correct. Any attention brought to the missing Mrs. Esther Warwick would bring the risk of discovery.

"I've hired a private inquiry agent, but he has found nothing more than one of Esther's friends saying she spotted her at Varney's Ices with a young woman the last day I saw her."

Audrey rested her gloved hand on the back of a chair before the desk. "Varney's Ices?"

"Yes. Esther's friend did not know who the woman was, and when she greeted Esther, apparently my wife dismissed her as a stranger." Doctor Warwick mussed his hair as he raked his fingers through. "Something has happened to her. I know it."

Hugh didn't want to be cruel; he could tell the doctor was going through hell. But there was a theory he could not overlook: "Esther walked out on her first husband. Who is to say she hasn't done the same with her second?"

True fury lit the man's face, incinerating the anguish and confusion. "To hell with you, officer. I know what you must think of her and of me, but you are wrong. Esther would never have left us."

Audrey picked up on that last word just as swiftly as Hugh.

"You have a child," she said.

All at once, the doctor's fury ebbed and again, anguish settled in his eyes. "Catherine. She is three years old. My sister is caring for her these last two weeks, but I know Esther would never leave her. Catherine is her world..."

His throat constricted, choking off those last words.

"Doctor Warwick," Hugh began, "had Esther mentioned anything about seeing old friends from Shadewell? Had she come into contact with anyone from there recently?"

He looked like Hugh had just asked him to consume something foul.

"Of course not. She would have told me."

"Or she would have kept quiet, so as not to worry you," Audrey replied. She had not told the duke about Delia, and Mary and Lord Rumsford had also held their tongues. But the doctor continued to shake his head, rejecting the idea.

"Esther knew how careful we needed to be. Living in Lambeth kept us a far step from her old home and life, but we could make no mistakes."

The doctor was not lying; he'd come forward with a criminal confession—falsifying the death of a woman in order to marry her himself—and yet he was standing firm on this.

"Doctor," Audrey said, tapping the back of the chair with a finger, her brow furrowed with thought. "Did you ever share with your wife the true identities of some of Shadewell's residents?"

When moments passed and his jaw firmed and lifted, Hugh anticipated the doctor's first lie.

"Don't bother to lie," he warned. "Only the truth is going to help you find your wife."

Though guilt eluded Warwick's expression, he did at least manage to appear chagrinned. "Yes. We have, over the years, discussed some of the others who were there while she was a patient."

At last. No patient folios had been rifled through; the doctor had provided all the intelligence necessary, however unwittingly.

Audrey turned to Hugh. "Mary met with Delia for ices. Varney's is quite popular."

If Esther had met with Delia, and then disappeared that same day...Delia's death was almost certainly linked to Esther. He turned back to the doctor.

"Delia?" Doctor Warwick came out from behind his desk. "Delia Montgomery?"

"Yes. Have you seen her recently?" Audrey asked.

"She was a patient," he replied.

"At Shadewell, yes, I know."

He shook his head. "No. Well, yes, there as well, but I meant *here*. Miss Montgomery was delivered in June, after she was arrested for indecent public behavior. It was only a short stay—she was repentant and agreed to several bloodlettings to relieve her of her hysteria."

Hugh grimaced. Thornton would have had plenty to say about the doctor's treatment of bloodletting—he thought it outdated and argued that rather than release ill humors, all it did was weaken a patient and make them listless and more ill. But Hugh was more interested in the fact that Delia had seen Warwick at Bedlam.

And then, shortly afterward, she began working with a blackmailer with knowledge of Shadewell's wealthier patients.

"Is your wife educated?" Hugh asked. "Can she read and write proficiently?"

Warwick seemed offended. "Of course. Esther attended a finishing school in Hampshire."

Hugh looked to Audrey, and she nodded. It was enough to go on for now.

"Thank you for your time, Doctor Warwick. If you hear from your wife, or learn anything more, contact me at Bow Street."

They departed the office and building, Hugh dragging in a deep breath of brisk autumn air as soon as they were crossing the entrance court.

"Esther penned the blackmail letters," Audrey said.

"Yes. But what could she stand to gain by this plot? You heard Warwick—they have needed to live carefully to carry out their false marriage."

For Christ's sake, Warwick had not even dared report her as missing. Any attention, at all, could undo all the lies upon which they'd built their life.

"Perhaps that is why Esther had Delia approach everyone in person and she remained hidden," Audrey suggested.

"And if Esther had decided to take on a new identity again,

perhaps with some new beau, she could have wanted a hefty purse to support them."

The pieces fit together, but something still bothered him. The child. Catherine.

"Why was Esther sent to Shadewell?" he asked.

They exited the gate, and Carrigan rushed to open the door to the carriage.

"That is exactly what doesn't make sense," Audrey replied, pausing before allowing Carrigan to help her up into the conveyance, where Greer waited. "Her infant son died. She was so distraught, she tried to take her own life."

"Why then would she leave her young child now?" Hugh asked, musing aloud.

Unless she planned to come back for the little girl. But then, why not take her right away? No, something was not aligning.

After a few moments of standing on the curb, pondering what they had discovered about Esther, a rustling wind sent the duchess's scent of camellia and rose toward him. She had held herself well during the interview with Doctor Warwick.

"What do you make of him?" Hugh asked. "The doctor, I mean."

She peered back at the asylum, of which they had been fortunate enough to only see the polished face of. The three stories of cells, females in one wing and males in the other, were a sight Hugh had tried to expunge from his mind.

"He seemed...human. Fallible." She turned her back on the place. "And yet still arrogant. The ruse they pulled on Mr. Starborough was cruel. Allowing the man to grieve his wife when she was not dead...it's heartless. How could they live with themselves?"

Hugh's bet was they had not lost a wink of sleep over the deceit. Had they been the sort to care, they would not have done what they had.

"It was inclination over duty, apparently," he muttered. "Delia and Esther were connected, there is no doubt. But I am not convinced Esther discarded Warwick and their child as readily as she did Starborough."

Audrey pressed one blond brow lower than the other, something she did whenever she was formulating some new stratagem—usually one Hugh did not like. "I could—"

"Go home to Violet House," he said, earning himself a powerful glare of contempt. "Please, duchess. I have to update the magistrate and put out a hue and cry for Esther."

Audrey's pensive frown reflected his own feelings of conflict in revealing Warwick's actions, but there was no getting around the fact that the doctor had committed a crime.

"Mr. Starborough will be crushed that his new marriage won't be valid," she said. "His wife is ill, he said. And he, too, seemed so aged. He used a cane for his limp and with his graying hair, he appeared so pallid. So forlorn."

"I am sorry for the fellow, I truly am. But to explain Esther's connection, I cannot leave out such important details." He'd already given the magistrate a chopped-up version of the duchess's involvement regarding the dead woman in the Thames; adding another lie to the story would eventually founder it.

She nodded primly and then took the driver's hand, climbing into the carriage. Hugh remained on the curb.

"I'll hail a hack," he said, even though he knew it was a risk not seeing her back to Violet House himself. She could go anywhere from here, and he noted that she had not agreed to return home.

"Where are you going?" he asked.

"I haven't yet decided," she replied, then addressed her driver to shut the door.

Carrigan did and, with a contrite glance at Hugh, got into the box.

"Liar," he grumbled as the carriage pulled away into traffic along Lambeth Road.

He turned around to search for a hackney or omnibus to hail. Luckily, a hack was approaching the pavement outside the brick walled courtyard. Hugh signaled the driver as he pulled the horses to a halt. The jarvey nodded to Hugh as he stepped down from the box to let out his current passenger. The man descended, his walking stick proceeding him, and paid the jarvey.

"Where to, guv?" the jarvey then asked Hugh.

He did need to go to Bow Street, but something weighed more heavily on him. "London Hospital," he instructed, and then hefted himself into the carriage.

CHAPTER
SIXTEEN

Carrigan came back around onto Lambeth Street a handful of minutes later. From her window, Audrey could not see any sign of Hugh. She felt slightly guilty about deceiving the Bow Street officer, but not enough to adhere to his request to return to Violet House. The quiet of the tomb-like home would be wretched. It was possible that Philip had returned from wherever he had gone off to, but if he hadn't, she refused to pace at home, worrying about him and getting angry—and she also refused to do the same while Hugh was actively searching for Esther.

She was not useless, and she also was not afraid of a little risk.

"Your Grace, are you certain I shouldn't come with you?" Greer asked.

While having Greer at her side would certainly be more proper, it would be much easier to move on her own. Her plan did not exactly include being forthright.

"I won't be long," she assured her maid as she removed her gloves and set them beside her on the cushion.

Carrigan handed her down to the curb, and though he did not approve, he said nothing. Neither he nor Greer could object to their mistress's decision, and she felt a bit guilty for that too. Surely, they were worried. Not only would being found entering Bedlam alone reflect poorly upon Audrey, but it would reflect poorly upon them. However, a woman was missing, and two more were dead, and so the narrow possibility that someone of influence or connection would see her, was not enough to hold her back.

She crossed the entrance court alone, her heart again leaping at an irregular rhythm. While she knew she would not be walking among the patients inside Bedlam, a heavy sense of sadness weighed upon her shoulders, even as she climbed the portico steps. It was as if the building itself emitted a stern somberness that penetrated right into the deepest recesses of her mind.

But as soon as the attendant who had greeted her and Hugh earlier appeared at the door to greet her now, she focused on what needed to be done.

"I'm so sorry," she began, "but I seem to have forgotten my gloves in Doctor Warwick's office. So silly of me, I know, but we were looking through some papers and I didn't want to smudge them with ink."

The excuse was pitifully weak, but she saw it through with a twittering laugh. The attendant indulged her with a grin. "Of course, ma'am. I will fetch them for you—"

"Oh no, I'm sorry, I haven't been entirely honest with you," she said with theatrical breathlessness and a look of pained remorse. "You see, there is also another matter I wish to discuss with the doctor that was simply impossible to broach with my brother present. It's...rather delicate."

She waited for the attendant's response with her pulse

thumping in her throat. He narrowed his eyes and frowned, but a moment later nodded. "I see. If you will wait in the doctor's office, I will find him and inform him of your return. I believe he is in one of the wards at the moment."

What providence! Audrey beamed at the young man, and she quickly made her way back to the office. If Doctor Warwick had still been there, she had a back-up plan, however hastily drawn. Asking the doctor for an item belonging to his wife would have been unbearably rude but backing down and giving up was out of the question.

Thankfully, as she entered the private office for the superintendent, all was quiet within. A room straight ahead looked to be a study of sorts, and to the immediate right was his office. To the left, a set of stairs led to what Audrey presumed to be Warwick's living quarters. After spying a lady's cloak and parasol hanging upon hooks at the first landing of the stairs, she was willing to wager he, Esther, and their child lived here. It wouldn't be entirely out of the ordinary—Doctor Warwick had lived at Shadewell in a wing closed off to the residents. The entrance to Bedlam was much the same. However, she couldn't imagine Esther would have been happy to live here, least of all with her child.

Thick carpet muted her footfalls as she climbed to the landing, and sure enough, she entered a foyer leading to a sitting room and dining room. A second set of steps led to a third level, where two bedrooms were located. Audrey entered the larger of the two, the furnishings and décor marking it clearly as Doctor Warwick's and Esther's. There was no time to spare. Doctor Warwick could arrive any moment.

Atop a dressing table, filled with lady's necessities, an ivory-backed hairbrush seemed the most likely object to retain memories. Esther would have used it often. Audrey crossed the room and, feeling as though someone was about to pop out and catch her snooping, picked it up by its carved ivory handle, inlaid with silver. She closed her eyes and opened her mind, immediately welcoming the image that appeared, clear and bright.

It had been years since she'd seen Esther, but she had not changed much. She had been petite; short and thin with delicate features. She appeared to be the same now, however as she brushed a lock of her golden blond hair, her chin quivered. Her eyes were glassy, the rims red. The room behind her, reflected in the looking glass, appeared to be empty. Had she and Warwick just had an argument? Or was she crying for some other reason? She was preparing to go out, it seemed. Audrey dropped her attention from Esther's anguished expression to the bodice of her dress. Silver satin, embroidered with blue thread, the capped sleeves trimmed with blue silk ribbon.

Impossible.

The gown was the one Audrey had cast off to Delia. The one Delia had been wearing when...

Cold shock poured through the veins in her neck and out along her arms. She dropped the hairbrush and the image scattered. The sound of the ivory, smacking against the mahogany table couldn't compete with the rush of blood pounding through her ears. Though she had tried to forget her visit to the bone house with Hugh and Philip, it came rushing back to her now. The body of the woman who'd been laid out on the table had been so badly bloated, her face had been unrecognizable. Audrey had identified the *dress*...not the victim.

Delia hadn't been wearing that cast-off. Esther had been. Esther, with her long blonde hair, just like Delia's...

With a sickening swoop of her stomach, Audrey backed up toward the door to the bedroom. Voices below stopped her in her tracks. A woman's voice carried clearly up the two levels of stairs.

"I cannot fathom why you would have allowed them to live here," she said sharply. "Here! At a lunatic asylum! I told you it was bad business, Stephen. You should have listened to me."

A lower, male voice was not audible, but she assumed it to be Warwick. He made some reply to what the woman said as Audrey's pulse streamed out in a panic. Heat built under her petticoats and chemise, and she bit her lip as she tried to concoct a believable excuse for wandering up to his private living area, should she be caught.

A child's voice was also muted. This had to be his daughter and the aunt the little girl had been staying with since Esther's disappearance. Audrey's heart sank. She hadn't just disappeared. She was dead. The unclaimed body on the table had to be Esther's.

So then, where was Delia? That she was in fact alive twisted up the whole case. It sent everything askew.

The voices became louder as she tiptoed into the hallway. A door led to a smaller bedroom—the one belonging to the child. Another door, likely to a closet. Audrey crept toward that one, hoping the newly built hospital would not yet have creaky floorboards.

"How could you expect a woman to agree to such conditions?" the shrill-voiced sister asked, alarmingly closer. Had she climbed the steps to the second level?

"Papa?" the little girl sounded uncertain, her voice warbling as if on the verge of tears. Audrey did not care for the way the aunt was speaking about the child's mother in front of her.

"Everything is well, button," Warwick said, his words clearer, perhaps out of anger. Then, in a lower tone, he said something stern to the aunt.

The door to the closet was open a crack; Audrey opened it further, praying for greased hinges, and backed into the space.

No sooner had she started to close the door than a cold object pressed against her throat. An arm grabbed her as a hand clapped over her mouth to stifle her yelp of surprise.

"Quiet," a voice hissed. "Or the little girl and the woman will pay for your selfishness."

CHAPTER

SEVENTEEN

Basil didn't see him right away when Hugh entered the ward. The valet was sitting in the chair next to Sir's bed, legs crossed, book open in his lap. He appeared to be reading aloud to the lad. When Basil caught sight of his employer, he closed the book and stood to greet him.

"Sir, am I relieved of my watch? I quite miss my regular bathing schedule. If the poor lad does not wake up on his own volition, I'm afraid my rather fragrant state might induce it."

Hugh arched a brow at the valet's blithe comment, and because he knew that Basil did, indeed, worry for the boy, suspected Sir had improved.

"He has woken up again?"

Basil nodded. "Once more, briefly. Mumbled something about *winning*."

Relieved, Hugh stepped closer to the bed. It had been five days now. His body had gone through a trauma and was recovering slowly. The fact that he was already so thin and battered likely made his healing more of a challenge.

"His mother has come in a few times." Basil rocked back

onto his heels, his hands clasped behind his back. He quietly added, "A fresh bruise on her chin."

Something would have to be done about the father. Hugh would have to find the man and take proper stock of him. See if he was just a bully with no one of his own size willing to challenge him, or something much more dangerous.

"We'll take care of that later. Soon, but later," he told Basil. "For now, I've got to get to Bow Street. I might have an idea who—"

"'S a lady."

The groggy, slurred words almost did not pierce the low murmur of the rest of the ward. Sir shifted his head on the thin pillow, eyes still closed. "Lady."

Hugh whipped toward Sir, then went to one knee upon the floor, gently placing his palm on the boy's shoulder. "Sir, are you awake?"

His parched lips broke apart. "Mister Hugh," he rasped. Basil called for a nearby dresser, busy changing another patient's bandages, to bring some water.

"Yes, I'm here," Hugh said. "Are you in pain? You've been out for days. I worried..." He didn't finish, realizing exactly what he'd worried: that Sir would not wake up. That the boy would die, that Hugh would have been responsible, and that he would keenly feel the empty space Sir left behind.

"Winning...she tried to..." Sir mumbled, his eyes fighting to remain open.

Hugh frowned "It's all right. Let me get you some water."

The dresser had brought a small cup and pressed it into Hugh's hand. He set the glass to the boy's lips. After some spluttering, at last, Sir's lashes parted. Hugh met the barest sliver of green irises and dilated pupil.

"Winnie," Sir rasped. Winnie, not *winning*.

"What's all this about Winnie?" Hugh asked.

"She were getting me a pie at Jim's cart," he said. Hugh nodded, construing that Winnie had been buying him food at a street vendor. Sir had claimed the ladies had taken a liking to him, and it seemed he had not been stretching the truth.

"Suddenly, she pulls me back. Points to this bloke and lady, arguing in front of a shop. Says the lady's her friend—" Sir broke off, coughing. He moaned and paled as he closed his eyes and tried to catch his breath.

"That's enough for now, gentlemen," the doctor said as he appeared at the bedside.

"Sod off. It's important," Sir said, sounding just as quarrelsome as ever. Hugh suppressed a grin. "Winnie calls her over, waving her arm, all excited-like. Calls her Delia."

An odd stroke of calm silenced Hugh's mind. He stood, his blood beginning to charge. "Delia? Are you certain?"

"As a nun."

Delia. She was *alive*? He tuned all his attention toward Sir. "What happened next?"

"Delia hears her name, sees Winnie n'me, and the bloke she's arguing with limps off—" He rasped a cough and breathed deeply, wincing.

The doctor shot Hugh a vexed glare. Hugh gently lifted Sir's head and touched the glass to his lips. The boy grimaced as he sipped slowly.

"I ain't no baby."

"Then stop complaining like one," Hugh replied, overjoyed to hear Sir griping.

He scowled but went on. "Delia motions Winnie into a passageway, like she wants to tell her a secret. I'm keeping my distance, remembering you said Delia washed up in the Thames. Anyway, she tries to stab Winnie." Sir closed his eyes again and took a few breaths. "I pushed her down, I did, but that witch moved fast. Got me before I even knew it."

186

Fury roiled low in Hugh's stomach. All this time, he and Audrey had believed Delia to be dead, a victim of murder. And yet she had tried to silence Winnie. Sir, too. And with Audrey's vision of a woman attacking Mary Simpson, and Sir's claim that Delia was swift with a knife, he was confident it had been her.

If the bloated corpse Constable Stevens dragged out of the river hadn't belonged to Delia Montgomery, Hugh now had a fairly good idea who it did belong to.

"You've done well, Sir," Hugh said, his throat tightening as the boy's expression filled with delight. Though no information, however integral, was worth risking his life for. Then again, Sir had been stabbed defending Winnie. No wonder she'd brought him to the hospital herself. She owed her life to him.

"Yes, quite brave," Basil said. Then cleared his throat at Sir's skeptical glance. A compliment did sound a bit off coming from the valet. "Perhaps a little reckless. Edging upon stupid."

Sir smirked, looking more comfortable with the insults.

"Just rest now," Hugh said. "You'll be able to go home soon. Your mother will be pleased to hear it—*Davy*."

Sir opened his eyes so wide, the whites of his eyes grew. Hugh barked a laugh.

"Now listen here, Mister Hugh, I can't have you calling me that—"

"Davy is a perfectly respectable name."

He groaned and whined, "It what me *mum* calls me," sounding more like a child than he ever had since he tried to pick Hugh's pocket and got caught.

"Very well, very well," Hugh said, stifling the laughter. "Sir it is. Sir David?"

"No!"

"All right, all right. Just Sir." He forced a serious tone. "One more question. The man you saw arguing with Delia. Did you catch anything about him? A name?"

Disappointment shadowed Sir's delight a bit. "No, and he weren't nothin' special; older, workhouse thin but wearing a fine suit. Bum leg. Had a face like a horse."

The description did not sound like Warwick in the least, but it still rang a few bells. He couldn't place why.

Hugh turned to Basil. "Stay with him. The woman, Delia, is crafty. I'll be back soon."

He was on the front steps to the hospital when he sorted out the description of the man Sir had seen. He'd said the man had "limped off" after talking to Delia. A bum leg. Audrey had mentioned the cane Mr. Starborough walked with that made him appear older than his years. And that he was not a hand-some man. A face, long and forlorn.

His pulse ratcheted up a notch. "Hell." Outside of Bedlam, a man had descended from the hired hack Hugh had approached. He'd had a walking stick, ostensibly, for a limp.

Esther Starborough's husband had found his wife's lover.

CHAPTER

EIGHTEEN

S he practically deserved the knife against her throat.

Audrey had dismissed the limping, cane-toting Mr. Starborough as a clueless, still-grieving widower, and now, she'd gone and backed into a closet that he was hiding within himself...waiting, it would seem, to wreak vengeance upon his wife's new husband.

How incredibly stupid could she have possibly been?

"What are you doing?" she hissed to Mr. Starborough, taking his threat against the aunt and child as seriously as the she did the blade poised at her throat.

"What I should have done the moment that devious woman contacted me to tell me of Esther's deceit."

The closet was pitch dark, stuffy, and warm, and Audrey could trace the odor of perspiration the wronged husband had been producing as he'd waited. Surely, he had expected Doctor Warwick to climb the stairs earlier, not her. He must have seen her and thought to stay put.

"Delia," Audrey whispered. "She did blackmail you after all?"

"How are you involved with her?" His grip on her tightened.

He'd wrapped his arm around her, and though he had not struck her as a particularly robust man, one did not need to be muscular to properly sever a carotid artery.

"I'm not involved with her," she replied, still quietly. The child and woman were her main concern now. Their voices still emanated from below.

"In fact, until just now, I believed Delia to be dead," Audrey added.

"The viper deserves no less."

Audrey could presume what had happened. "Delia went to you with the truth about Esther. Why? To blackmail you?"

The voices of Warwick, the child, and aunt seemed to grow louder and closer. They were on the second level; Audrey was certain of it. Her heart thudded. She wouldn't allow Mr. Starborough to harm the child.

"Not at first," he replied. "No, at first, she only told me because Esther had betrayed her. Delia was running some extortion scheme and had pulled Esther into it. I should have seen it coming, but all I cared about was Esther, that she was alive. She'd betrayed me, let me believe..." He hushed as emotion constricted his throat. The blade shifted and pressed harder. Audrey felt a hot prick of pain.

"I didn't believe the woman," he went on after regaining some control and lightening up the press of the knife. "So, I followed her. And there she was...Esther. My Esther. Alive. All this time."

Mr. Starborough began to shake, the tremors in his body affecting the hold of his blade. Audrey squeezed her eyes and prayed he didn't accidentally nick her throat. She tried to hear whether Warwick was still present downstairs, or perhaps coming up to the third level. But all she could hear was the soft hiss of Mr. Starborough's voice in her ear.

"I didn't mean to. The fury...I've never felt anything like it."

Audrey opened her eyes to the darkened closet. She could see nothing, and yet she also had a clear vision of what had occurred when Mr. Starborough had seen Esther, alive and well.

"You killed her," she whispered, her throat dry.

The back of the corpse's skull had been shattered by a blunt object...a walking stick?

"She was supposed to be dead...drowned in a bog." Anguish thinned his voice. "And she acted as if *I* had done something wrong by discovering her secret. As if...as if my questions, my confusion aggrieved *her*."

"You didn't intend to," Audrey led him, wanting to calm him before he slipped and cut her throat.

"No, I didn't, of course I didn't," he hissed.

There were no voices coming from below now; they had either heard them and gone still or left the private apartments.

Mr. Starborough had lost control when faced with the depth of Esther's betrayal. And could Audrey blame him? The heartless woman had allowed him to suffer so that she could be happy. It had been indefensibly selfish. And wrong. But she had not deserved to die.

"You are not a killer, Mr. Starborough. Losing control once doesn't make you a cold-hearted murderer. But if you kill Warwick, you'll hang."

"You think I care about that?"

Surely, he believed he had lost everything already. But she sensed she could sway his mind with a little bit of hope.

"Warwick is going to be arrested," she said. "A Bow Street officer knows what he and Esther did. It is illegal. He'll be punished. He is going to lose everything. Cooperate and the magistrate may well show you lenience."

She had no earthly idea if that was true, but at that moment, she would have said nearly anything to calm him.

"Delia is the true killer," she added. "Not you."

If Esther was the woman from the Thames, that meant Delia was alive. She had not been used in this extortion scheme —she'd been the driving force behind it.

The woman Audrey had seen when she'd held Mary Simpson's ring...it had been Delia. Mary must have seen her and known she was not dead. Could that be why she had wanted to come to Violet House that day? To tell her? Before she could, Delia had silenced her.

"Help me find Delia," she went on, sensing Mr. Starborough's indecision. "She needs to be stopped."

"You are right. I don't want to kill you." The blade disappeared from her throat, though his hand stayed latched around Audrey's arm. "But I also cannot let Bow Street take me."

He jerked her arm and before she could wonder at his intentions, a sharp blow to the side of her head rocked through her. It wiped out all sound and feeling, and all she knew was the folding of her legs.

It felt as if she were falling forever, never landing upon the floor, but sinking through it. Down and down, she spiraled, ears muffled against sound, eyes cemented against light. And then, all went still.

A throb of pain at her temple and an excruciating thirst was what finally forced her eyelids to open. It was a chore. She wanted quiet, stillness, peace. And yet, deep inside, she knew she could not have those things. Not just yet. There was something to do. Something important, but the details eluded her.

The stiffness in her legs and arms became impossible to ignore. With a groan, she tried to move. Slowly, she remembered. The closet. Bedlam. Warwick. *Mr. Starborough.*

Jolting awake, Audrey realized her dry tongue was caused by a ball of fabric that had been stuffed into her mouth and wrapped around her head. Starborough had not only gagged her, but her ankles were tied, and her wrists too, behind her back. The door to Warwick's third-level closet was firmly closed; it was utter blackness within. How long ago had Starborough left? Carrigan and Greer...they had to be still outside, waiting. Worrying. How long until they came looking for her?

Audrey wriggled on the floor, trying to position herself onto her knees, something that might have been more easily done had she been wearing trousers instead of a dress. The humiliation of being trussed up like a sow and shut away in a closet tempted to overwhelm her. She had to keep her wits. Taking a deep breath, she gave up trying to get onto her knees, and rolled onto her back instead, arms pinned beneath her uncomfortably. Tucking her knees in toward her chest, she used the motion to rock herself forward. Before she could flop back down again, she twisted to the side and landed on one elbow.

Below, the sound of an opening door and low male voices caused her to freeze. Warwick? She burned with anger and mortification. If only she could get herself out of this bind without help! Audrey continued to strain into a sitting position. Until one voice climbed above the others.

"Audrey!"

Her heart stuttered, then leaped. It was *Hugh*.

She tried to shout his name, but it was nothing more than a muffled scream. What was he doing here? Writhing in both embarrassment and the need to stand, Audrey continued to scream through the gag. She managed to get onto her knees, but with her ankles pinned together she couldn't stand as she normally would.

"Audrey!" Hugh called again, his voice clearer as it traveled up the stairwell. She slammed her shoulder against the door, needing to make some noise to draw him up.

As she was about to slam her shoulder against the wood for a fourth time, an ache blooming, the closet door fell away. Audrey toppled out, onto the floor in the hallway.

She lay on her back, looking up into Hugh's alarmed face. She was both overjoyed to see him and utterly mortified.

"Audrey? What the devil?" He ripped the gag from her mouth, untying the knot at the back of her head.

"Starborough." Her mouth was as dry as sawdust and the word came out as little more than a rasp.

He touched her temple and grimaced. "You're hurt. Starborough did this?"

Her head throbbed but that was the least of her worries. "Esther. She's—"

Warwick appeared on the steps and Audrey bit her tongue. It seemed Mr. Starborough had not done him in after all.

Hugh nodded. "I know," he whispered, then set about untying her wrists and ankles.

"You do?"

"Sir. He told me it was Delia who stabbed him. She's alive, and so..."

Audrey nodded, understanding that they had each come to the same conclusion. Though to tell Warwick now would be premature.

"What in hell is going on up here?" the doctor asked, a look of pure mystification upon his face. "Miss Haverhill, an attendant said you were waiting for me, but what are you doing in my private rooms?"

"Doctor, it's a complicated story and there isn't much time," she said, extending her hand to Hugh. He took it and helped pull her to her feet. She wobbled, the hallway tipping a little bit.

"Someone from Bow Street will be calling on you soon," Hugh said, "but we must go."

Doctor Warwick looked between them, a hopeful glint in his eye. "Is this about my wife? Have you found her?"

Though it had been a wretched thing to deceive Mr. Starborough as they had, Audrey could see that the doctor did truly love his wife. He would be devastated when he learned the truth. But now was not the time.

"There is a lead," Hugh provided, and then bid him goodbye.

He and Audrey hurried down the stairs, back through the office door, into the hospital's main corridor, and past a puzzled attendant.

"It was Mr. Starborough who killed her," Audrey said as they descended the steps.

Hugh slowed his pace as alarmed glances met them across the entrance court. "I suspected. Though I expected to find him in Warwick's office, not you, floundering on the floor like a fish."

Audrey gaped at him, her lips chapped and her injured, possibly bloody, temple likely the true cause of the looks of shock meeting them. "I was not floundering!"

"Then what was all that thumping around I heard?" Hugh replied, taking a coy sideways glance at her.

She was scowling at him when she thought of it: *thumping*. Audrey stopped walking, the gated lodge just a few steps away. Hugh turned back to her.

"What is it?"

When she'd been at Mr. Starborough's home, there had been a thumping sound from the upper level, as if something had fallen over. He'd blamed the sound on his new wife, and the maid's eyes had widened as he then asked Audrey to leave. But what if the maid had not been reacting to his rude behavior toward a caller? What if she'd stared at him in that way because he'd been *lying*?

"He doesn't have a new wife."

"Come again?" Hugh asked. Audrey shook her head, certain of it now.

"Delia. I know where she is."

NINETEEN

The bruise on Audrey's temple had started to turn a sickly bluish purple as Carrigan drove them back over the Lambeth Bridge and toward Kilburn. She appeared slightly bleary-eyed, like constables at the Brown Bear who imbibed one or two too many pints. Fussing over her injury would have only made her cross, so Hugh kept his comments limited to her heedless decision to sneak back into Warwick's office and snoop through his private rooms.

"If I had not gone back to Warwick's office and held Esther's hairbrush, I wouldn't have seen her wearing my cast-off gown and realized *she* was the body from the Thames."

"Something I readily—and *safely*—deduced when Sir woke and told me Delia was the one who'd attacked him."

She'd ignored him and added, "And if I had not run into Mr. Starborough—"

"You mean if he had not held you at knifepoint in a darkened closet."

"—then I would not have put together that Delia was at his home," she continued.

"*Might* be at his home," he corrected. "That was yesterday, was it not?"

The woman could have gone anywhere. If she'd been there at all.

Audrey sat back and gingerly touched her temple with her ungloved fingertips. She winced. "Yes, well, it is at least a place to begin."

"Your Grace, if I may," Greer said, and produced a kerchief for her mistress's still weeping wound.

"I'm well, Greer, truly," the duchess replied, though she accepted the square of linen and dabbed at the blood. The regard Audrey showed for her lady's maid was evident in the way she thanked her with a small grin. There were too many members of the ton who treated their staff with indifference, but not Audrey. It was one of the first things he had reluctantly admired about the duchess.

"We will check the home, and if she and Starborough are not there, we are going directly to Bow Street to put out the hue and cry for them both." Hugh tucked his chin and stared her down. "Are we in agreement?"

Audrey lowered the kerchief. "Did I hear you correctly, Officer Marsden? Did you say *we*?"

The delighted lilt of her voice gave him momentary satisfaction. However, the prospect of walking into the magistrate's building with the duchess did not give him the same feeling.

"I did, but do not grow attached to the idea, duchess."

She pressed her lips against a grin but failed to mask it. They continued toward Watling Street and soon, Audrey announced they were close. She slid forward a little on the seat, as if in preparation for Carrigan to stop and let them out.

"You are staying in the carriage, Your Grace," Hugh said, and before the mulish woman could so much as part her lips and make her argument, he held up a finger. "I am not asking. I am telling. This is dangerous. Delia killed Mary with hardly any effort, and she nearly killed Sir. If she is in there as you suspect, I cannot apprehend her while worrying for your safety. So please, Audrey, for once do as I ask and *stay in the bloody carriage*."

Her mouth popped open and yet no sound emerged. She simply stared at him, unblinking. Her maid, to her right, wrinkled her forehead in surprise too. Silence filled the inside of the carriage as Carrigan whistled to the horses and brought them to a stop. Hugh had never seen the duchess speechless before; he rather liked it.

"Very well," Audrey replied belatedly as the driver dismounted. The chassis shook. Hugh opened the door himself, one eye still on the duchess. He didn't quite believe her, but she appeared surly rather than falsely sweet and placating.

"Keep an eye on the house and if you see or hear anything untoward, holler for a street patrol." He jumped to the curb and took the short front walk to the door. Just as he was about the reach for the brass knocker, he noticed the inch-wide gap between the door and the jamb. It was already open.

Hugh pushed the door open a little wider, and when no sound met him, peered in.

A woman lay on the floor just inside the entrance, crumpled around the legs of a credenza table. Hugh rushed inside and drew his flintlock. Crouching next to the woman, he felt her neck for a pulse. She was alive, but the blood on her brow looked to have come from a deep gash at her hairline. A mobcap hung askew off her plaited bun, and based on her plain dress and pinafore, he assumed this was a maid.

He stood and listened for any indication that the attacker was still in the house. For several moments, there was nothing but his own thumping pulse. And then, a muffled grunt, like a man being pummeled in the gut. Hugh's eyes darted toward the staircase and the first landing. He crept up the steps, hoping the carpeted boards would absorb his footfalls. There were no more errant sounds, though his instinct knew that he was approaching a confrontation.

At the landing, rooms stretched left and right, with several doors closed. Only one was open. Cautiously, Hugh moved toward it. With this flintlock ahead of him, he entered, tensed muscles ready for whatever met him.

But no foe leaped at him. Instead, he found a man seated across the room, on the floor, his back lined up against the wall. He pressed his palm to his chest attempting to staunch the flow of blood. It wasn't working. Blood soaked his shirt and hand, and more viscous crimson liquid spluttered from his lips.

"Starborough," Hugh said. Dimly, the man registered that he was not alone. He peered up at Hugh with a blank look of confusion.

"Where is Delia?" Hugh asked.

A whisper of movement behind him, and a rush of premonition racing up his back, were his only warnings. Hugh spun on his heel and took aim at a woman who stood too close. At the same time, hot pain pierced his forearm. A shot fired off before the muscles in his hand went utterly slack. His flintlock clattered onto the floor, and the woman swiped her leg out, sending his dropped weapon spinning away, out of reach. In another shock of pain, she ripped free the blade she'd plunged into his arm, and then slashed at his face. Hugh leaped away, avoiding all but a nick across his cheek.

The woman brandished her blood-stained blade, a wild grin stretching her lips.

"Delia Montgomery," Hugh said as he clutched at his quickly numbing arm.

"Audrey's dear Runner." She grinned inanely. Her dress, far too elaborate for anything other than a ballroom, was stained with speckles of blood. Tendrils of blonde hair had escaped her pins and hung in her eyes.

"Why have you done this?" he asked as sharp bolts of pain began to tear through his arm.

Delia twittered a laugh. "Which part? Gutting Estelle's husband here? Well, it was me or him. He came at me with his cane, the same way he went at Estelle. But I'm faster." She jiggled the long, thin blade that she gripped with ease.

"You didn't kill Mary Simpson in self-defense." A surge of nausea cramped his stomach and beads of sweat dotted his brow and between his shoulders. His arm was wounded seriously, much worse than a mere stab. Had she cut an artery? He needed to subdue her and get the knife from her hand before Audrey or Carrigan came running; they had surely heard the report of the pistol. But his right arm, his dominant arm, wasn't cooperating. He could barely flex his fingers.

"Bad luck for Mary that she saw me at Varney's. Couldn't have her telling anyone, not when I was supposed to be that bloated corpse."

When she smirked at the state of Esther's dead body, Hugh comprehended that this woman was vacant of any feeling, any morals. There would be no reasoning with her.

"I suppose it was *bad luck* when Winnie saw you too." His pulse pumped harder at the memory of Sir's near death, which only made his arm ache more.

Delia shrugged and said nothing. It wasn't worth anything to her, it seemed. Hugh attempted another approach.

"Esther wrote the letters."

At the mention of her, Delia grew amused again. "She was more than willing, after I saw her at Bedlam and learned she'd married *wicked, wicked Warwick*," she said, singing the name as the older woman at Shadewell had.

Warwick had known what former patients Delia could

blackmail. He had shared the names with his wife, who had, in turn, shared them with Delia—because Delia had been blackmailing Esther too.

"But Esther changed her mind," he led as blood continued to weep from his arm. His vision fuzzed, then sharpened again. One show of weakness, and this viper would strike. He backed up slowly, closer to Starborough, whose walking stick lay upon the floor beside him.

"Got cold feet. She didn't believe I'd tell her poor sod of a husband the truth about where she was." Delia pinned her lips like some maniacal imp.

"Cheating innocent people didn't sit well with her conscience. Imagine that."

"*She's* the one who cheated! Got herself a new life. Why couldn't I do the same?"

"Esther didn't kill anyone in the process." Hugh's heel knocked against the dropped walking stick. Delia didn't notice. Her earlier humor had flashed over to anger.

"Only because she had it easy. Had everything handed to her. She went from one wealthy husband to another."

"Her baby died, and she went mad. In what way is that easy?" Hugh argued, if only to keep Delia agitated, to hinge her attention on anything but his foot, nudging the walking stick up onto the toe of his boot.

"Oh, poor Esther, as if dead babies don't happen every day." Delia rolled her eyes. Hugh used the moment to hitch his knee up, propelling the walking stick into the air. He caught it, but black dots flooded his vision, and before they cleared, the walking stick was ripped from his hand. Delia tossed it behind her.

Wild, cackling laughter grated his ears. "Oh, look, the Runner's about to faint!" Delia stepped closer with her knife. "Now, do I let you bleed to death, or do I—"

Delia stumbled forward, then crashed to the floor. The Duchess of Fournier stood behind her, Starborough's walking stick in her hand and a look of awe at what she had done painted across her face. She dropped the walking stick as Carrigan ran into the room on her heels. The room tilted and blurred as Audrey rushed forward, gaping at the blood on his sleeve.

"Your arm!"

"I'm fine," he said, but he wasn't. Damn it, Delia likely *had* cut an artery. "Carrigan, find something to bind her arms and legs before she wakes, and call out for a street patrol."

"We heard the gunshot. Greer is already fetching the police," Audrey said as she shrugged out of her spencer and came to him. "Give me your arm."

"I told you to stay in the carriage."

His head swam as she wrapped his bloody arm up into her fine lady's coat. It would be ruined, and he meant to say as much, but instead, he repeated himself: "I told you to stay in the carriage."

"Instead of harping on my disobedience, you could thank me for saving your life," she said as distant police whistles sounded.

A chiming in his ears preceded a swirl of lightheadedness, and Hugh suddenly found himself on his back, with the duchess hovering over him.

"Hugh? Oh, god, Hugh? Wake up! Carrigan, help!"

"I'm awake," Hugh whispered, and then, a tide of sense smacked into him. "Hell. Audrey, you must go. *Now*."

"But you're hurt—"

"You can't be here when the street patrol arrives. There is no way to explain your involvement—"

"I'm not leaving you."

Hugh forced himself up onto his left elbow. "Woman, you are going to be the death of me. Carrigan, get her out of here."

The driver finished with the blanket he'd ripped from the bed to hastily tie Delia's wrists and ankles. "Your Grace, he's right. You must leave."

Audrey grabbed hold of Hugh's coat collar with both of her hands and fisted the material. "Don't you dare bleed to death, Hugh Marsden."

She pressed the collar down, smoothing it with her palms, fretting over him. Then, with tears sparkling in her eyes, got to her feet.

"I will go to Thornton's," he assured her. She nodded and allowed Carrigan to steer her to the door. "Audrey."

She jerked back toward him.

"Thank you," he said. "That was quite a swing."

"Yes, well, I was quite vexed."

Carrigan urged her again, and the duchess fled.

TWENTY

As soon as she returned to Violet House, Audrey stripped off her dress, with Greer fussing over her in a most-unlike-Greer way. She must have brushed up against Hugh's wounded arm for she'd ruined the material with his blood. So much of it. But the man was far too stubborn to die. Audrey kept telling herself that for the entire ride home, and Greer had assured her of it as well when Audrey had spoken the mantra out loud.

Nevertheless, she charged their butler Barton to send a footman to Thornton House to inquire if Lord Thornton had yet seen the Bow Street officer, and if so, how he was faring. Worry plagued her as she'd plunged into the hot bath that her maid had drawn for her. Only after she had toweled off, dressed, and allowed her hair to be put into a haphazard braid did Greer announce that Philip had returned home.

"When?" she asked, jumping to her feet.

"While we were out, Your Grace."

Though she was irked at Greer's delay in letting her know, she understood the reason for it. To have rushed headlong into Philip's room or study to confront him while she was wearing a bloodied dress would have been shocking for the duke.

Gathering herself up, she stalked through the boudoir, to the attached sitting room within Philip's bedchamber. No matter how much she wanted to fling the door open and enter his room like a tempest, she held herself in check and instead moved with what felt like glacial poise.

The drapes were pulled, cloaking the room in darkness. A single lamp on his bedside table produced a circle of light around him as he lay in bed. Grayson, his valet, straightened from the bedside abruptly, a bottle and spoon in his hand. Without a word or a look in her direction, he took his leave.

Philip, propped against some pillows, turned his head toward her. His skin, ashen and waxy, turned her stomach. Dark shadows bruised his under eyes.

"What has happened to you?" She stepped forward. "Where have you been?"

Her fury all but vanished at his wretched appearance. She had seen him after days-long absences due to opium, but he had returned looking sloppy and confused, not like this. Unless he had found a new vice.

"I know we quarreled before I left for Northumberland, but for you to leave no word for nearly three days, and while a murderer was targeting their blackmail victims...how selfish could you possibly be?"

Philip closed his eyes and sighed. "It isn't what you think."

"Then tell me what it is because at the moment, I'm fearing the worst."

He gestured for her to come sit next to him on the bed. Audrey assented but only perched on the edge. She then crossed her arms and waited.

"I have been to a doctor."

"A doctor?" The beginning of their summer in Hertfordshire

came back to her in a rush. They had barely arrived at Fournier Downs before Philip had come down with a severe malaise, one he could not escape for nearly a month. "Are you ill again?"

"It is...connected," he said. "This was a private consultation and treatment from a physician at Lock Hospital."

She held herself stiffly. Lock Hospital wasn't as infamous as Bedlam, but its reputation was certainly known. It was not a hospital people readily admitted to visiting.

"For obvious reasons, I could not be seen there," Philip continued, "so I took a room at Grillion's Hotel for a few days and had Doctor Bagley attend me there."

After months of agonizing over any possible scandal that would further corrode their reputation, to be seen setting foot inside Lock Hospital, known for its treatment of venereal diseases, would have been catastrophic. And to be attended to here, with a full staff of servants, also unwise.

"What are you ill with?" she asked after a moment. She'd had her suspicions, especially after the spell last June, and when Philip replied, his throat constricted, she realized she'd been correct.

"Syphilis," he replied, so soft it was barely a whisper. "Grayson was the only one who knew I was at the Grillion, and why. I ordered him to remain quiet, even from you."

Audrey felt no resentment or anger toward his valet; the man had lied outright to her, saying he didn't know where the duke had gone off to, but his loyalty to Philip was to be admired.

"What sort of treatment?" she asked.

Syphilis was not uncommon; in fact, if rumors among the ton were anywhere near the truth, the disease ran rampant among them. And if the upper crust of society suffered in large numbers, who knew how many more among the middle and lower classes were afflicted.

It was a debilitating disease, one that flared and receded, but in time, could cause horrendous problems. Shadewell had been a place to convalesce for a number of men and women suffering from it.

"It's called mercury salivation," Philip said, then, a shudder wracked his body. Audrey uncrossed her arms and reached for him. He held up his hand weakly. "No, it's fine. I'm fine. It seems my body rejects even the name of the treatment now. Don't ask me to describe it, you will be utterly appalled."

It was his gray pallor and weakened state that appalled her, however. "Was it truly that horrible?"

"Worse than what you are probably even thinking," he replied, but then tried for a grin. "Doctor Bagley says it is supposed to be a lasting cure."

She took his hand and squeezed. "Why didn't you tell me? I was worried. I thought..."

"That I had fallen into my old ways?" He squeezed her hand in return. "I am sorry. You're right. I should have told you, but darling, I was ashamed."

Where he had contracted the disease was no mystery. He and Lord St. John had been lovers until the dissolution of their relationship and the murder of Miss Belladora Lovejoy. Before that, he'd been addicted to opium, and he could have shared relations with someone else then too. He did not have clear memories of that time. While she had been angry with him for the opium and for carrying on in secret with St. John behind her back, it was not a bitterness she could cling to now.

"Don't be ridiculous. You never have to be ashamed of anything with me," she said, unexpected tears biting the backs of her eyelids.

"You are far better than me, in everything. I am weak."

"You are human."

"You're my very best friend, Audrey. And I have failed you. Time and time again."

Tears now spilled forth, dampening her cheeks. "Now, stop that. You must rest. Tearing yourself down is not going to help you heal."

He shook his head with a limp motion and slurred some his words as he said, "I want you to be happy. I want you to have the things I can't ever give you. Maybe I was hasty in suggesting we think of a child..."

It was either exhaustion governing his tongue, or perhaps some of the remnants of the mercury treatment. Now wasn't the time to have any sort of deep or serious conversation about their marriage. Or about the topic of adoption.

"We will sort things out in time, Philip," she said, standing from the side of his bed. "But right now, you must get well. That is all that matters."

She released his hand, which went to the mattress like a rock. He closed his eyes, and she took light steps back toward the sitting room and her attached boudoir.

"Your case," he said, causing her to trip to a stop. She turned back toward him. "The investigation. What happened?"

There was too much to tell him, and he was half asleep as it was. She forced a grin, even as a lurch of worry over Hugh's arm turned her stomach. "Solved. I will tell you everything in the morning."

He nodded. "Good. You're safe then?"

"I am."

A moment later, his breathing became more rhythmic. Audrey left his room and crossed to her own, wishing Philip *had* been holed up in an opium den these last few days.

She'd have preferred it to the truth.

AT THE FIRST blush of dawn, Audrey was still awake, her eyes burning and mind tumbling. Her footman had returned from Thornton House the previous evening with word that Hugh's arm had been seen to, and that he was on the mend. She had grappled with whether to go to St. James's Square herself or perhaps even to Bedford Street, but she had resisted. Barely.

Not knowing what had happened to Delia after she and Carrigan had collected Greer and hurried away from Mr. Starborough's residence had plagued her throughout the night. Her mind jumped between thoughts of Hugh, to combing through all the signs she had missed regarding Delia, to Philip's illness.

She checked in on the duke a handful of times, only to find him sleeping. Grayson sat vigil. Not needed, she returned to her room, only to pace the carpet. Finally, at dawn, she dressed and extended her restless pacing to the rest of the house. With the duke ill in his bed, it would be unseemly for her to quit the house and seek out Hugh—even Greer would disapprove. So, she remained, though she felt bound by the walls around her.

By late morning, Audrey sat at her desk, certain that Violet House had in fact been trapped in amber, which was slowly hardening and closing them off to the rest of the world for all time. Sunlight illuminated the dust motes drifting through the study's silent air. The clock ticked steadily closer to noon. If there was no word by then, she would send a footman to Bedford Street. No, to Bow Street. That's where he would be. Blast all the constables who would tease Hugh! She needed to know what had happened with Delia.

But perhaps he wasn't there. He might be at his home, recovering from his wound. She lowered her hand to the desk and drummed her fingers against the wood. Needing to move, Audrey pushed herself up from the chair just as a knock landed on the study door. She froze and fixed a neutral expression upon her face. "Come in."

Barton appeared within the threshold. "Officer Marsden from Bow Street is here, Your Grace. Are you at home?"

Audrey straightened, instantly released from a feeling of confined torment. "I am," she said, her fervor utterly appalling.

Audrey turned her back to the door, not wanting Hugh to see her eager face as soon as he entered. She tried to regain some composure, but with the lack of sleep and stretched-thin patience, it eluded her. Her butler announced Hugh, and she reluctantly turned.

She bit her lip at the sight of him, his right arm tucked up into a sling. "Your arm—"

"It's fine. Or at least it will be." He winced as he flexed the fingers on his right hand. "Thornton says the blade sliced through some tendons and nerves, and nicked bone, but with rest, it should heal."

A knot loosened in her stomach. "Thank goodness. When you fainted, I was afraid it was more serious."

"I did not faint," he said, his voice clipped.

She bit her lips together against a grin. "Of course not."

He let out a long exhalation and tossed his hat onto a couch cushion. "Starborough is dead. He would have hanged for killing Esther, of course, but I think a hanging would have been a bit quicker."

Audrey had seen Mr. Starborough's slumped figure in the upstairs room, the vast amount of blood upon him. However, at the time, closing in on Delia without being heard or seen had been of more urgency.

The gunshot she'd heard from the carriage outside had kicked her into action, and though Carrigan had tried at first to bar her from entering the house, he had eventually given up. She'd grabbed one of the walking sticks from the urn near the unconscious maid in the entrance foyer and had immediately rushed upstairs. She'd barely drawn breath until after she'd swung the walking stick, cracking it against the back of Delia's head.

"And what of Delia?" she inquired.

"She woke in her cell at Newgate."

Perhaps she ought to have felt some relief to learn that she had not dealt her a killing blow, however now, the possibilities for complications and exposed secrets began to mount and tangle.

Hugh took a few strides toward the desk where Audrey still stood. "She has admitted to killing Starborough and Mary Simpson, and the attempted murder of Sir."

Audrey frowned. "Has she? But what of the blackmail? And Esther and Dr. Warwick?"

"I've informed Warwick that Starborough killed Esther after finding out the truth that she was alive all this time. He was devastated, to say the least." Hugh scowled. "Though, I find it difficult to feel sympathy for him."

Audrey nodded; she understood what he meant. The only person she truly felt sympathy for was Esther's little girl, Catherine, who was now motherless. An innocent victim in all of this.

"And the blackmail?" she asked. Here, Hugh's brow pinched. If Delia revealed that she'd been blackmailing the Duke of Fournier, it would all unravel. The police would learn of Audrey's stay in Shadewell. Even if she claimed it was false, that Delia had been lying, the damage would be irreparable.

"Your involvement is limited to the dress Esther was wearing at the time of her death. One she received from Delia, who got it out of charity. She's agreed to say she only black-mailed Mary Simpson and Esther Starborough."

Audrey shook her head, confounded. Last night, Hugh had ordered her to run before the police arrived, to avoid her being caught in scandal. And all night she'd been awake, her mind restless, but not once had she considered what Delia might say when she woke.

"Why would she agree to that?" she asked.

Hugh lowered his voice. "I offered a bargain, and she took it."

"What bargain?"

"She has a child. One she gave up to St. Bailey's Orphanage but planned to get back once she had the money to support him. I offered to arrange for her child to be withdrawn and placed in a boarding school for orphans instead. There's one in Hammersmith. He'll be given an education and when the time comes, an apprenticeship somewhere." He lifted a shoulder in a show of nonchalance. "It was more than she could ever do for him now, and she knew it."

For a moment, all Audrey could hear was the soft ticking of the clock. Hugh's rich brown eyes watched her carefully, as if he was waiting for her to say something. But her mind was curiously empty. At the moment, all she could do was feel crushing self-reproach.

"You would do that?" she whispered, though not by choice. Her throat cinched tight, trying to subdue a sob. Her eyes, however, had no such stopper. They began to sting again. Hugh was essentially making this child his ward, providing the funds to see him through an education and apprenticeship, all to shield Audrey and her secret.

A line creased the space between his dark brows. "Of course, I would."

Her eyes grew hot and blurred; she shook her head and turned from him. "You shouldn't," she rasped, furiously blinking, and swiping at her wet cheeks.

Goodness, how she hated crying in front of him. In front of anyone, really, but especially him. And not because he would use it against her in any way, or shame her for it. No, she didn't want to cry because she suspected exactly what he'd do next.

"Tell me why I shouldn't," he replied, and blast him, she'd been right. He'd come closer.

She sealed her eyes shut and breathed deeply. Moments like this when he wasn't arrogant or argumentative, but instead tender and vulnerable, were dangerous. In these moments, she could nearly convince herself that what she felt for Hugh wouldn't eventually bring them both pain.

"It isn't your responsibility to protect me."

Hugh stayed at her shoulder, his nearness heating her back and raising the small hairs along the nape of her neck and arms. "You are not a responsibility, Audrey. I *want* to protect you."

"That is for my husband to do." Bile touched the back of her throat. She hated herself in that moment. Hated having to push him away with cruelty. But it worked. Hugh took a step back; she felt the gap of cold air at her back.

After a moment of silence that stretched for an age, he spoke, his voice low and bitter. "He's been doing a splendid job of it lately, hasn't he?"

Audrey whipped around, despite her wet eyes and cheeks flushed with shame. "That isn't fair. He's done what he could."

"How?" Hugh tucked his chin and glared at her. "By rolling over, showing his stomach, and paying his blackmailer?"

"You can't blame him for not having the same resources as you. He's a duke. He can't go chasing blindly after criminals!"

His eyes rounded as she realized she'd backed herself right into a corner. "You're a duchess, and yet you do!"

Audrey's lips parted, but a retort dried up on her tongue. She sealed her lips and smoothed the front of her dress. "I simply mean to say that the duke did what he could to protect me from scandal."

"And where was the fine duke yesterday when you were nearly killed at Bedlam?"

Hugh's question struck like an iron fist to the stomach. Audrey tried not to flinch. "I was not nearly killed."

Her temple had scabbed. It was a minor wound. Nothing compared to Hugh's arm.

"Where was he?" Hugh pressed, as if knowing she was avoiding the question.

"In bed. He has fallen ill again."

Hugh's furious expression softened. "I see."

A chill shivered from her crown to the small of her back. *Did he see?*

The ire slowly drained from his tensed shoulders, and he raked his fingers through his hair. "How serious is it?"

"I'm not sure," she answered. "He is being treated."

He met her gaze. Though he said nothing, she could read his questions. His suspicions. He was no fool. And the wry lift of his brow whispered that he didn't believe she was in the dark about the duke's illness.

"You know what it is."

It wasn't yet noon, but Audrey's body was strung tight, and when her eyes landed on the decanter of whisky on one of the bookshelves, she gave in. She crossed the room and poured herself a drink. Then splashed some into a second snifter. She extended it to him and held her breath as he came toward her to accept it.

Hugh lowered his voice. "Are you well?"

Her lips lingered on the glass, the smoky scent of the whisky touching her nose. "I?"

"These things are transferred in one way," he said, harsher than before. He clenched his jaw and took a sip of his drink. She mirrored him, and only spoke after the liquid burned a path down her throat.

"I am fine. Philip loves me, but not in that manner." She looked into her glass; it was easier than looking into Hugh's perceptive eyes.

"Never?"

Audrey looked up. Warmth crept into her cheeks. "Philip and I agreed on certain terms. You are an intelligent man, Officer Marsden, I believe you can gather what one of them was."

As soon as she called him by that name, she regretted it. It was a wall of defense. A way to separate herself from him. It only made her feel worse.

"I understand." Hugh flexed the hand bound in the sling as he sipped his drink. Then, after a heavy silence, asked, "What were the other terms?"

She stared at him. It was an incredibly bold question, asked without a note of cunning. Only curiosity. Audrey didn't owe him an answer. In fact, it would be completely within her right to tell him to leave this instant. But she found that she didn't want to.

"That we would always be honest with each other. We would discuss everything. I suppose...we were both looking for someone to trust. A true companion and friend."

It had been thrilling to have a friend, at last; someone who wouldn't judge her or want to change her. It was something she'd never had. She and Philip had found a way around the traditional pathways of the ton and had reveled in their cleverness.

"I wouldn't have to marry Bainbury, and Philip would have a wife he did not need to conceal anything from. There would be no need to pretend. We agreed on everything. Everything was going so well..."

"Until he started keeping secrets," Hugh said.

Audrey wasn't sure if it was the whisky loosening her

tongue or the long, sleepless night. Or perhaps it was the impression of being isolated from the rest of the world here in her study. But she hazarded an honest reply. "So am I."

Hugh was quiet a moment. Then guessed what she meant. "The kiss."

She dared to look up at him. "I must tell him."

It was not like in August, when they had only stood close on the quarry ledge, each of them knowing what the other wanted to do. Audrey had already chastised Philip for not being honest with her; she wouldn't be a hypocrite now.

Hugh drained his drink. "You've already assured me he won't call me out. Even though he thinks I am *unsuitable.*"

Heavens. Audrey had hoped Hugh would forget that conversation, but it seemed he stored every detail in his trap of a mind. He set the empty snifter on the shelf next to the decanter.

"However, you never said what he thinks I am unsuitable for," he drawled. She glared at him. Was he teasing?

"It is obvious. Don't pretend otherwise."

He stared at her with such intensity that the tips of her ears burned. Hugh took a step closer. "I want to hear you say it."

She gaped at him. "Why? To humiliate me?"

"Never. I only want to watch your lips form the words."

Shock and thrill poured through her. Something she had never felt, something unruly and wild, took hold in the pit of her stomach, in the narrow space between her hips. Breathing became arduous; her eyes seemed to adhere to his, and she was drowning beneath them.

"To be my lover," she whispered.

He continued to hold her stare. "I cannot be your lover."

Audrey steeled herself against the immediate pang of disappointment. She lowered her eyes to the glass in her hand, longing to melt into a puddle of shame. "I didn't ask you to be."

"You didn't need to. I can feel it. Just as you can feel how much I want you."

Clear, coherent thoughts refused to align in her mind. All she could hear were those last words. She must have appeared mute and stupid as she stared up at him, trying to comprehend.

"But you said—"

"That I could not be your lover. Not that I did not want to be."

Audrey gazed at him, completely bewildered. She closed her eyes and turned away from him. Why must he make things so complicated? "Well, just as I said before, I haven't asked you, and I don't intend to."

"Good." His voiced punched. It slashed at her as cruelly as Delia's knife.

She spun to face him. "You should leave."

Hugh stood back, his hand dropping to his side. The hand of his injured arm clenched into a fist. "You're angry."

"You assume too much, Mr. Marsden."

He put up his uninjured hand in a gesture of surrender. Then, went to the sofa and retrieved his hat. He turned the brim in his hand, then said, without looking at her, "I wouldn't be satisfied with only half of you. It is all of you I desire. No less. And since that is impossible, I must put it out of my mind."

She held her breath as he started for the door, her ears beginning to chime.

"Hugh." His name slipped out before Audrey even knew what she was going to say. She could think of nothing. Her sole objective had been to stop him from leaving.

He paused at the door. "Thank you."

Audrey frowned. "For what?"

"Saving my life. You were right, I should have thanked you."

She recalled her complaint in Mr. Starborough's home. It seemed petty now.

"Yes, well, you've saved my life a few times. I suppose now I've saved yours too. So that means we're square." She was babbling. If any of it made a lick of sense at all, it would be a miracle.

Hugh only laughed and shook his head. "No more dead bodies, please."

"You make it sound as if I will them into being."

"*Audrey.*"

She parted her lips, the amusing diversion of squabbling allowing her to breathe again. But then, it was gone.

"Goodbye, duchess." It sounded final, and her throat knotted again.

Hugh left before she could utter a word. Before he could look her in the eye.

No more dead bodies.

As Audrey stared at the study door that Hugh left open in his wake, she wasn't at all certain she wished for the same thing.

THANK you for reading Silence of Deceit, the third Bow Street Duchess mystery! Please leave a rating and review on Amazon to help more readers discover the series. Keep reading for a sneak peek at Penance for the Dead, the fourth Bow Street Duchess mystery, releasing June 3, 2023 and available for pre-order now!

PENANCE FOR THE DEAD
A SNEAK PEEK AT BOW STREET DUCHESS
BOOK 4

Chapter One

March 1820
Saturday Night

The stale, stuffy air inside Lady Reed's ballroom reeked of floral perfume, cologne, and dank undernotes of sweat. Audrey waved her silk fan in rapid beats in front of her face, attempting to disburse the overpowering scents. Outside, winter clung on with freezing temperatures and icy gales, and while she didn't particularly care for the blustery cold, Audrey would have happily leaped into a snow drift right then if it meant escaping the ballroom—and the presence of Lady Minerva Dutton.

The dowager countess had been valiantly attempting to corner Audrey and Philip, the Duke and Duchess of Fournier, and Philip's younger sister, Lady Cassandra, ever since the three of them were announced into the ball. Knowing the older woman's penchant for gossip and for making thinly veiled cuts, Audrey had tucked Cassie close to her side and weaved between guests, evading her. Cassie had only returned to London a few weeks ago. She'd spent the last several months in Sweden with some of Philip's trusted friends—Mr. and Mrs. Olsson, one of Philip's former Oxford professors and his wife, who had moved back to Stockholm. They had graciously taken in Cassie when she'd found herself in a dire situation last summer. Unwed and with child, she had needed a place to have her baby, far away from the eyes and ears of polite society. Should anyone learn of her predicament, she would have been thoroughly ruined.

Unfortunately, Lady Dutton was as keen as a hawk when it came to spotting scandals. Cassie's absence had sparked the countess's interest. Though the ball was something of a crush, and she'd successfully eluded Lady Dutton for the past half hour, Audrey's luck ran out at the punch table. For the last several minutes, the countess had not relinquished her hold.

"But enough about this party's ill-advised décor," she trilled after commenting at length on Lady Reed's decision to outfit the four corners of the ballroom to reflect the four seasons. "My dear Lady Cassandra, I am still waiting to hear how your aunt is faring."

Cassie, who had slipped a little closer to her elder brother, gave no reply. She seemed to freeze under the woman's scrutiny. Philip had sipped his punch slowly during the woman's tiresome monologue on proper ballroom décor, his expression impassive. Now, he cleared his throat.

"Our aunt has made a full recovery, thank you for inquiring," he said.

Cassie had, allegedly, forgone the Little Season last autumn to remain in Scotland with her ailing great aunt, and to recover emotionally from the turmoil at Fournier Downs last August, when Lady Charlotte Bainbury had been killed. After Philip's own arrest and scandal earlier that spring, it seemed only natural that the young woman would choose to wait for the proper Season to make her bow. However, in reality she had given birth to a daughter. And almost immediately after, had said goodbye to her.

Lady Dutton flashed a grin. "I'm so relieved to hear as much, Your Grace. Tell me, Lady Cassandra, did you have any opportunity to socialize while you were there? I recall Lord Hartford saying he and his family were in Edinburgh for Michaelmas. Did you not see them?"

Audrey met Philip's eyes as she took a sip of her punch. By appearances alone, Cassie did not look any different than she had in the summer. However, there was a seriousness to her now that had not been present before. The old Cassie would have waved a hand through the air and spun some excuse with a light laugh and clever remark. This new Cassie looked as dismissive and sour as Philip.

"No," she answered sharply.

Lady Dutton's forehead wrinkled above arching brows.

Audrey smiled, though the expression was wooden. "The duke's aunt resides outside Glasgow. It's rather rustic and out of the way."

"I see," Lady Dutton said. Audrey only hoped the woman did *not* see.

Only family knew of the truth; it had been impossible to keep it from Philip's brother Michael, Lord Herrick, and his wife, Genie. Genie would undoubtedly write letters to Cassie in Scotland, to which Aunt Hestia would reply with the truth— that she was not there. And if any of Cassie's friends wrote to her, Aunt Hestia needed to know to redirect the letters to Sweden.

Their dour great aunt had been scandalized, but she'd agreed to protect the family name. Michael had blustered and threatened to kill Lord Renfry, the blackguard who'd seduced and abandoned his sister, but then, like Philip had, he'd grudgingly agreed keeping the truth from Renfry would benefit them all. The man had stooped to seducing his own stepmothers, the Earl of Bainbury's second and third wives, and neither Philip nor Michael wished for their beloved sister to be married to such an ingrate. Tobias, their youngest sibling still at Cambridge, was the only one who did not know the truth.

Audrey snapped her fan shut. "It is quite a change of pace being back in town after so long in the country," she said, attempting to formulate a reason for her sister-in-law's sullen attitude. "Cassie does so enjoy the fresh air."

Cassie forced an anemic response. "Yes, it is quite overwhelming here."

Audrey's chest tightened with sympathy. Cassie had not said much about the birth, or of handing her newborn over to Mrs. Olsson, who'd found a loving home for the child, but she was clearly heartbroken. And seeing Genie and Michael's new baby, George, had likely been salt in a wound. Little George, now nearly five months old, was a round-cheeked, black-haired, little angel, and even Audrey was not immune to pangs of maternal longing when she held him.

Lady Dutton simpered. "I never marked you as a country girl, Lady Cassandra. Perhaps your newfound love of the countryside is the reason your correspondence while away was so...irregular?"

The letters would have traveled from London, to Scotland, to Sweden and back again, causing quite a delay. It had not gone unnoticed, it seemed.

"Either that or my sister grew weary of dull conversation. A sentiment I share, completely," Philip said, more agitated now.

Lady Dutton's eyes narrowed at his implied barb.

"If you'll excuse us, my lady," he said, and then took Cassie by the arm and stepped away. Audrey quickly followed.

"She won't have anything kind to say about you now," she whispered to Philip once she was by his side again.

"Has she ever?"

"The woman is a wretch," Cassie added, and Audrey could not disagree.

"Perhaps we should take our leave soon," she suggested.

None of them had wanted to attend Lady Reed's soiree to begin with but snubbing one of the most important events of the Season had not been an option. The Duke and Duchess of Fournier hadn't received many invitations during the Little Season, as they'd still been entrenched in scandal. First, Philip had been accused of a gruesome murder, one from which he'd been exonerated, but it had still damaged his reputation. And then, two murders on the grounds of their country home, Fournier Downs, had threatened to drag them back into disgrace.

Getting back into society and introducing Cassie properly was expected. With any luck, it would also begin to repair the Fournier name.

But not if Philip continued to be such a bad-tempered bear.

Cassie stopped to say hello to a few ladies she was acquainted with, and Audrey and Philip fell back, near one of the many tall windows lining the walls of the vast room. The glass radiated cold, and Audrey longed to press her cheek against it.

"Are you feeling unwell?" Audrey asked him after a moment.

He had undergone a second mercury salivation treatment the previous week, and it had left him bedridden for three days. His first round of treatment had been in the fall, and though the physician had told him it would completely cure his syphilis, Philip had become unwell in January with what he called a "flare", though he refused to elaborate on the symptoms to Audrey, who needled him out of pure concern. Once he was feeling well again, Dr. Bagley from Lock Hospital had met him for another treatment. He still appeared pale, his cheekbones more prominent than usual.

"I am fine," he replied, then with a sigh, added, "Just a little tired."

Audrey took his arm. To the rest of the *ton* currently in the ballroom, the action would look like a wife taking her husband's arm in loving affection. And while Audrey did love Philip, and he loved her, it was not in the traditional sense. They were the best of friends now that they'd been wed three years. Audrey often wondered if she and Philip might even be closer than many of the married couples surrounding them. So often people married for alliance, for money, for titles and position. She and Philip had married for convenience, too, but with the mutual understanding that theirs would be a marriage based on friendship. That didn't mean they did not have their hiccups. The one that immediately, and often, came to her mind had a name: Principal Bow Street Officer Hugh Marsden.

It had been several months since she'd seen him, and since they'd been in lockstep while uncovering a deadly blackmailing scheme that involved Audrey and a few of her former acquaintances at Shadewell Sanatorium. When they'd pinned down the culprit and arrested the deranged woman, Hugh had made sure Audrey would not be connected to the asylum in any way. He'd been true to his word. The last five months had been normal to the point of becoming dull. Considering his status as a Bow Street officer was well below her own rank as duchess, there was no acceptable reason for Audrey and Hugh to see, or so much as bump into, each other.

She missed him. The yawning ache in her chest whenever she thought of him was proof. Perhaps, if another few months passed, and then a few more, that ache would begin to lessen. Audrey wasn't certain if she looked forward to that, or if she dreaded it.

Her only link to Hugh was Lord Thornton. She would not have even that had she not grown so weary of daily monotony that she decided to attend a scientific lecture at the Lyceum. It wasn't entirely unheard of for ladies to sit in on such lectures, and when she saw an advertisement in the paper for an exhibition and address on fossils of prehistoric sea creatures, she'd been unable to stay away. She'd taken her maid Greer as a formality and had chosen two seats in the back of the hall. The male attendees had all noticed them, of course, and had whispered amongst themselves. When one of them stood and came to greet her, Audrey's heart had started racing. Lord Thornton was Hugh's closest friend, and as fourth son of a marquess, had decided to make his way in the world as a physician. He'd welcomed Audrey to the Lyceum and offered to sit with her and Greer, then afterward, introduce her to a few of the more "accepting" men of his acquaintance there.

Audrey had since attended several lectures, and Lord Thornton had been at most of them. He'd discreetly let her know that Hugh's arm, which had been seriously injured in early November when they had captured the murderous Miss Delia Montgomery, was recovering nicely. That he was busy as ever at Bow Street, and that Sir, the young street urchin-turned-errand boy who was devoted to Hugh, was also doing well after his own stabbing, also at Delia's hand.

"Come," Philip said, interrupting her thoughts. "Let us say our goodbyes to Lady Reed."

He and Audrey rejoined with Cassie and found their hostess near the springtime corner of the ballroom. Garlands of faux green leaves cut from crepe wove through a trellis studded with bright yellow and red silk daffodils. A mass of cottony clouds hung suspended from the ceiling. It was truly garish.

Lady Reed sipped a glass of punch, ignoring the women on either side of her. She stared into the crowd, her brow pinched. In fact, it took the clearing of one of her companion's throats before she noticed the duke and duchess had joined them. With a start, Lady Reed turned toward them, blinking.

"Oh, Your Graces, forgive my distraction," she said, quickly setting the punch glass on the tray of a passing footman. Audrey noticed the slight tremor of her hand, the punch nearly splashing over the lip of the glass.

"Is all well, Lady Reed?" Audrey asked. The older marchioness, her steel gray hair stylishly upswept with framing curls, again seemed to startle.

"Yes, quite," she answered shortly before falling awkwardly quiet.

"We wanted to thank you for your hospitality before we take our leave," Audrey said after a moment.

"My wife feels a megrim coming on," Philip said before the marchioness could ask why. Audrey, still holding Philip's arm, covertly pinched him through his evening jacket. A megrim! She wasn't prone to megrims in the least; however, it was a reasonable excuse.

"Oh, how disappointing," the lady said. If her attention had not roamed toward the crowd again, Audrey might have believed her. But she was clearly distracted. Concerned, even.

"Thank you for attending, Your Grace," she said, her eyes flicking back to the duke. She then canted her head toward Audrey. "Your Grace. I do hope you are feeling better—"

Lady Reed broke off just as a strange, foul smell wafted under Audrey's nose. Behind them, voices raised with alarm. Audrey turned to find a grayish haze quickly filling the room. Men and women nearby covered their mouths and noses with their gloved hands, coughing.

"What in the world...?" Philip was cut off as he began to hack on a cough too. Audrey covered her own mouth and nose, but the sharp, sulfuric odor of the smoke slipped between her fingers and stung her nostrils.

"Cassie!" Audrey cried as her sister-in-law began to cough wildly. Philip gave her his handkerchief and wrapped his arm around her. The crush of guests, panicking now, began to surge toward the ballroom doors. With watering eyes, Audrey pulled on Philip's sleeve to stop him from joining the masses. They would only get bottlenecked at the doors.

"This way!" she shouted above the sudden clamor, and her husband redirected Cassie as he followed Audrey toward the back of the room. A pair of glass doors had been shut against the cold air, but during a stuffy spring soiree, the doors would have been thrown open to an airy veranda.

Audrey navigated through the thick smoke, her throat beginning to burn, her eyes streaming with tears. She wasn't the only one who'd thought of the back veranda as an escape; at least a dozen others had already reached the haven. The doors were open and a small crowd had gathered on the stone veranda, their dress shoes and slippers swallowed by a few inches of slushy snow. Audrey gasped for air, relieved to be free from the smoke. Her throat and eyes still stung, and by the red, teary eyes all around her, everyone else was just as afflicted.

"Philip," she gasped, when she saw him doubled over, still coughing. Cassie had quickly recovered and now gripped her brother's arm, rubbing his back as the convulsion passed.

The dozen or so others on the veranda shivered in distress, all of them speaking at once.

"Is the ballroom on fire?"

"What was that foul smoke?"

"I think my throat is bleeding!"

The smoke had certainly seared Audrey's throat too, but she didn't taste blood, thankfully. Inside, the smoke was so thick, it indeed looked like something had caught ablaze, but there were no flames, and the smell was not the familiar one of burning wood. It was chemical. And yet, it was familiar too, though Audrey couldn't place how.

"Now we must walk through the snow, to get to the front of the house," a woman bemoaned.

"I will go around," Philip rasped. "Cassie, Audrey, stay here while I fetch Carrigan. We will carry the two of you—"

"Don't be absurd, it is only snow," Cassie said, and Audrey was happy to hear a bit of her high spirit again.

A short, grating scream from inside the ballroom split the air. Everyone on the veranda went quiet. It hadn't been a scream of panic, but of pain and surprise.

No one moved. Audrey, however, could not remain where she stood. Someone had been hurt. She tore Philip's handkerchief from Cassie's fingers and, covering her nose and mouth, plunged back into the smoke.

"Audrey!" both Philip and Cassie shouted after her. She didn't stop. The smoke engulfed her, but if she squinted, she could peer through it a bit better. It still burned her eyes, but as she hurried deeper into the ballroom, the brume lessened.

A sharp prick of pain in the center of her foot startled her to a stop. She gasped and immediately lifted her foot to see what she had trod upon. Attached to the sole of her slipper was a small metal object. She plucked it out and saw it was a sort of charm—three golden leaves spread out like a fan—and that the sharp post backing it had pierced her foot.

Audrey tossed the offending thing aside and returned to searching the room for the person who had screamed. "Hello? Is someone injured?" she called.

She stopped abruptly again when a figure on the parquet flooring became visible through the smoke. It was a woman. She lay prone on the floor, face down, arms thrown out beside her. She wasn't moving.

"Audrey!" Philip barked, and a moment later, he grabbed her arm. "What the devil are you doing?"

He saw the woman and swore under his breath. She and Philip approached, but instantly, Audrey knew it was too late. A dark pool of blood had started to creep out from around her torso.

"Help!" Philip called between gasping coughs as Audrey stared at her in shocked horror. "Someone, quick! A woman is hurt, help!"

Within seconds of Philip's shout, men came forward through the dispersing haze. Audrey snapped out of her shock and quickly kneeled beside the woman. Her face was turned, her cheek to the floor. Her eyes were half open, but flat. She was certainly dead. *Killed.*

Before the oncoming men could see her, Audrey reached for the woman's hand. With her gloved hand, she slipped off the simple ring the woman wore on her right index finger.

"*Audrey*," Philip warned under his breath, knowing exactly what she was doing.

With the ring, Audrey could apply her most unusual ability to read the memories of objects, to see into their recent past. Perhaps, she could find out who had hurt this poor woman. It had to have been someone at the soiree. The smoke...had it been a trick to clear out the room and set upon her, unseen?

She closed her fingers around the ring and stood as several men, including Lord Reed, joined them. Philip pulled her close to his side.

"We heard a scream from the veranda," he explained. "Her Grace and I found her like this."

Lord Reed bent to peer at the dead woman. "Lord Beckett," he called sharply to another man with him. "Send for a constable at Bow Street."

Audrey's heart slowed, then streamed out a few extra beats. But then Philip spoke, stilling her pulse.

"It would be best if the officer you fetched wasn't Officer Marsden," he said to Lord Reed.

Audrey turned to gaped at him. "Why ever not?"

He couldn't possibly want to restrict Hugh just to keep him from her presence.

"Quite right," Lord Reed said gravely. "If I'm not mistaken, this is Lady Eloisa Neatham."

Gooseflesh rode up her arms and down her spine. Audrey stared at the dead woman with new shock. Eloisa Neatham left London years ago after a salacious scandal, where her half-brother was accused of ruining her.

And her half-brother was none other than Officer Hugh Marsden.

Unravel the unexpected mystery behind Officer Hugh Marsden's scandalous past in Penance for the Dead (Bow Street Duchess #4), releasing June 3, 2023. Available for pre-order now!

ABOUT THE AUTHOR

Cara is an author, history lover, and Netflix junkie. She loves to read and write across genres, but her heart is reserved for romantic historical fiction and mystery. When she's not writing, she's freelance editing, driving her kids everywhere, burning at least one side of a grilled cheese, or avoiding doing laundry.

ALSO BY CARA DEVLIN

The Bow Street Duchess Mystery series

MURDER AT THE SEVEN DIALS

DEATH AT FOURNIER DOWNS

The Sage Canyon series

A HEART WORTH HEALING

A CURE IN THE WILD

A LAND OF FIERCE MERCY

THE TROUBLE WE KEEP

A Second Chance Western Romance

Made in the USA
Coppell, TX
09 May 2023

16606001R00142